HOUSE
at the
END
of the
SEA

VICTORIA M. ADAMS

ANDERSEN PRESS

First published in 2024 by
Andersen Press Limited
20 Vauxhall Bridge Road, London SW1V 2SA, UK
Vijverlaan 48, 3062 HL Rotterdam, Nederland
www.andersenpress.co.uk

2 4 6 8 10 9 7 5 3 1

British Library Cataloguing in Publication Data available.

ISBN 978 1 83913 423 4

Printed and bound in Great Britain by Clays Ltd, Elcograf S.p.A.

For Faith, my child of two worlds

1

Breakwell

'There's a boy spying on us from the beach,' said Milo.

Saffi didn't turn around. She fixed her gaze on her brother seated opposite her at the picnic table, and waited. Behind him, southwards along the town's promenade, waves rushed almost to the sea wall. Milo seemed too small to her in his green shirt with a T-rex on the front, poking at the dregs of his milkshake with a straw. A picture of innocence.

Except, he was lying. She knew that.

'He's got something.' He had a worried look. 'I think it's a gun.'

She held his eye. 'Stop it, Milo.'

'Turn around. You'll miss it.'

'Just once, I'd like to sit quietly and wait for Dad.'

'It's true, I swear.'

It wasn't. Milo's tales had started right after the funeral and showed no signs of stopping. The grief counsellor said: *Your brother lies because he doesn't want to accept a reality without his mum.* Saffi wished it was that easy to change reality.

'Please.' He was squirming with frustration. 'Look!'

He sounded so desperate that she finally glanced over her shoulder. All she saw on the beach was a slim figure in a brown jacket. There was no way of knowing if he had been 'spying'. Otherwise, the shore was deserted apart from birds. There were a great many of those, wheeling and turning over the bay.

'Too late,' said Milo.

Sun, kids crying over dropped ice cream, the burnt-sugar smell of candyfloss. That was how a seaside town should be, Saffi thought. But not this one. This one couldn't even manage a summer. It was August but the breeze felt more like October. The promenade had one post office that sold crisps and cards, one tea shop named Betty's where the owner hung sad, useless sun-catchers in the window. The lines of groynes on the sand resembled grinning teeth. And they were going to live here. They had to leave London and everything they knew behind, move in with Grandma and Grandad in this nowhere place at the edge of the sea, all because Mum was gone and Dad couldn't manage Milo alone. Anger sat in a lump in Saffi's throat.

Just then, a gull landed on a nearby table with a scrabbling thud. Milo watched it jab at the wood with its yellow beak.

'Seagulls evolved from velociraptors,' he said. 'Know that?'

The gun was forgotten. He had on his serious *I read this in a book* face. Saffi fought the urge to scream.

'Careful,' said a voice from behind. 'They can be mardy, those ones.'

Saffi looked round to find a boy her own age, about

twelve or thirteen, watching them from the terrace. Freckled and blond-haired, he could have sprung up out of the grey stones for all she knew. She hadn't seen him arrive. His hands were thrust in the pockets of a leather jacket; the T-shirt underneath might once have had a Leicester City logo. His trainers were tied with nylon string, pale green. He lifted his chin to indicate the gull.

'Snatch chips right off your plate,' he said.

Saffi shrugged. 'He hasn't bothered us.'

But she wondered if the newcomer would. He was edging towards them, hands still in his pockets, an eye on the gull. The bird stared at him sideways as if it didn't think much of him, either. Then it heaved itself in the air and flapped off. The boy relaxed a little.

'Weren't you the one spying on us from the beach?' asked Milo.

It might have been. But Saffi didn't see how the boy could have reached the terrace, if so. There were no stairs. He didn't deny it but withdrew one hand, holding it out to her.

'I'm Birdy,' he said. 'Birdy Lythe. You here on holiday?'

Saffi wasn't used to talking to strangers in the street. She hesitated before getting up to shake his hand.

'I'm Saffi. This is Milo. We just moved here.'

'Oh, aye?' That surprised him. 'Where from, London?'

Saffi nodded. 'And you?'

'Breakwell, born and bred.' He pointed across the bay to a line of white bluffs. 'My dad runs a park up by Flamborough.'

That was where Grandad and Grandma lived, in a B&B

at Flamborough Head. Saffi realised that Birdy's 'park' must be nearby. She wasn't sure if she should say so.

'Sounds nice.'

'Well.' He scuffed the pavement with his foot. 'I guess. I mean, there's lots to see round these parts. Stacks, arches, smugglers' caves . . .'

'Caves?'

Milo's question was breathless. He had scrambled up from the bench to peer at the boy, hooked by the tourist pitch. Even Saffi felt a reluctant tug of interest.

'Heaps.' Birdy warmed to his theme. 'Big ones at North Landing. But you can find 'em all over. And shipwrecks.'

'Shipwrecks?' Milo's eyes grew round.

'I'll show you if you like. I know places.'

Saffi was suddenly afraid this boy with green laces would offer his tourist-guiding services, then ask for money. Or just ask for money.

'It's kind of you,' she said in her most formal London voice. 'We'll be fine.'

An instant later, she felt mean for saying it. Birdy only smiled, as if he didn't care one way or the other.

'Saf.' Milo turned to her. 'D'you think Dad'll take us to see a shipwreck?'

'You know Dad. If it was an Iron Age dig, maybe . . .'

But Milo wasn't listening. 'My grandma and grandad have a B&B in Flamborough,' he told Birdy, eager.

Saffi realised, too late, that he had spilled her secret. Birdy didn't miss it. A frown settled on his face.

'What d'you say your last name was?' He was staring hard at her.

'I didn't.' *Here we go*, she thought. 'It's True.'

Birdy must have recognised the name, for he seemed bewildered. 'True? But you don't look—' he began, before biting his tongue.

Saffi felt a familiar weariness. People always saw Mum's Iranian side in her, never Dad's English one. It annoyed her because she couldn't even speak the language. She had no idea what Mum's aunts and uncles and fleets of cousins were saying when they pinched her cheeks and cooed in Farsi. She opened her mouth to make a sharp rejoinder. But Birdy spoke first.

'Trues. Figures.'

Saffi could tell he didn't mean it as a compliment. 'Why?'

Before he could answer, she felt the air move. With a great flap and flurry of wings, a seagull – she didn't know if it was the same one – swooped down on them from above, so close that its webbed feet almost grazed Birdy's face. Instinctively, he raised his arms. There was a breathless moment as the gull hovered over him, an angry grey-white blur, yellow beak agape. Then, as quickly as it came, it went. Birdy didn't look surprised. He flicked a downy feather off his jacket.

'Told you. Mardy,' he said.

He appeared to have made up his mind about something, however. His grey eyes, which were pretty for a boy's, ringed with dark lashes, lingered on Saffi.

'Nice to meet you,' he added. 'Sorry I can't stay. Enjoy Breakwell.'

With that, he strode away along the promenade, leaving Saffi and Milo staring after him in shock.

'But what about the caves?' Milo was crestfallen.

Saffi didn't know what to think. It was strange: the way the boy spoke, the way the gull behaved, how both left so abruptly. She gazed after the receding figure, unsure whether to be relieved or disappointed he was gone. Birdy was the first person her age she had met in Breakwell, on this or any other visit. He would probably attend her new school in September. She wished she hadn't been so short with him.

That was when she noticed the birds. It wasn't just gulls patrolling the promenade. It was all sorts – sparrows, crows, magpies, a type of white bird with a yellow head she didn't remember the name of. More arrived as she watched, flapping and fluttering down to the terrace. And they were all staring at her. Fixing her with beady eyes. The whir of their wings filled the air.

It lasted for a frozen, impossible second. Saffi looked at the birds. The birds looked back. Wasn't it meant to be *birds of a feather flock together*?

The sound of her name distracted her. Dad had exited the tea shop across the road, a familiar figure in a tan jacket, waving. When she glanced back, the birds were gone. Only two gulls remained, fighting over a chip. Milo was already running to meet their father. Saffi shook off the dull trance that had come over her and followed. She must have imagined it. Birds wouldn't do that. She was tired, half-asleep after the long drive.

'Who needs that French Riviera,' Dad remarked as they joined him. 'When we have all this.'

He was gazing out at the grey-brown sea, much as Saffi had done. Nine times out of ten, when Dad said something, it was to make a joke. She loved that about him. But today the quip fell flat. He looked grim, as if he had an unpleasant task weighing on him. From this angle, moreover, she grasped how Birdy had arrived on the promenade. There was a set of steps behind a blue bin.

'You OK?' she asked.

'Eh?' Her father tore his eyes from the view. 'Taking care of your old dad, I see. I'm fine. Been a long drive.'

Then he put one arm around Milo and one around Saffi, drawing them close.

'Listen, you two,' he said. 'I wanted a word before we arrive. Your grandparents are old and set in their ways. It'll be *stop your maunging* when you skin your knees, or *don't be such a wuss* when you're scared of the big horse.' He winked at Saffi. 'But that doesn't mean we change. We look out for each other. Wingmen?'

He held out his fist, expecting a bump back. It was something he had done since they were both tiny, but it felt strange and out of place on the chilly seafront. Milo didn't respond. After a pause, Saffi gave Dad's fist a tap with her own.

'Wingmen,' she said.

'There's caves in those cliffs.' Milo pointed to the headlands. 'Where smugglers would hide stuff. Can we go?'

'North Landing. I'll show you one of these days. Come on.' Dad led them to their blue Skoda at the kerb. 'Wouldn't want to miss your gran's tea.'

He was joking again. Grandma's cooking was terrible. Saffi remembered that much from their last visit two years ago, as well as the incident with the horse. Every time she came here, something like that happened. She fell off a horse, or got stung, or met a boy who decided he didn't like her family name. Welcome to Breakwell-by-Sea. As Dad started up the engine, she fell to mulling over their old life in London. The cramped flat in Battersea, the friends she would probably never see again. All those people who had once known Mum. Who looked at her now with faces full of sympathy.

Saffi hated that look. She wanted to tear up the past two years and stamp them in the ground.

With a movement so habitual she hardly noticed it, she reached up to touch the silver star pendant under her T-shirt collar. Mum's gift. It was because of her name: Tara Persephone, 'Saffi' for short. Tara meant 'star' in some old language nobody spoke anymore. Another one she didn't know.

A star for my little star, so you'll always come home.

That had been the last gift.

Now, home was Breakwell. Grey, hostile, full of rude boys and seagulls, a place she didn't much remember. As far as she could tell as they drove on, the town consisted of no more than a few streets, fronted by grey terraces or ominously shuttered-up chip shops. On the outskirts, brick bungalows gave way to fields. They passed a clutch of cottages then the entrance to a stately home. After that, Dad turned onto the main Flamborough road, a dual carriageway bordered by hedges.

'Who'll call the towers?' he said to the children. 'Go!'

Saffi remembered this bit. Grandma and Grandad's house was so lonely on its wooded promontory, so engulfed by trees, that it became a game to spot the chimney stacks. Those were the 'towers'. She could see the first turn-off ahead – green on green, easy to miss. But Dad knew his way, barely slowing to swerve to the right. *No Horses*, she read on the asphalt. Why weren't horses welcome? Then they were in another world, far from chip shops and bungalows, plunging down a lane through a tunnel of trees. The setting sun shone in bursts, lighting up the trunks.

They reached the bottom of a ravine, splashed through puddles, climbed up again towards the headlands. A tell-tale lightness glimmered between the leaves, a glimpse of open sky. Saffi found herself holding on to the edge of her seat. Even Milo was excited, nose and palms stuck to the windowpane.

Then he crowed: 'I see them. I see the towers!'

This time, it was true. Saffi made out a smudge of white, the red of a chimney. Dad turned onto a gravel drive bordered by rhododendrons. A plaque on the gate bore the name, *Fortune House*. Even though she had seen it all before, she had the strangest sense that nothing would be the same after this visit. They had passed some point of no return – though for good or ill, she didn't know.

The drive snaked on, grey gravel glistening with wet. A few moments later, her grandparents' home appeared: a large, double-fronted Victorian villa, painted white with a brick trim around the windows. These were dark and narrow in the evening light and had always reminded Saffi of a row of mouths. When she was smaller, she used to wonder if the house was going to eat them. But as they drew near, the place looked more like a big sandcastle with its pale walls and crenelated top. It was only when her father pulled up beside it, killing the engine, that the view from the promontory became visible.

Fortune House was flanked on three sides by woods. Oak, sycamore and beech trees stretched mossy arms up to the sky. On the fourth lay emptiness. The house sat perched on a high cliff above the open sea.

2

Fortune

'You must be famished,' said Grandma, waiting at the door to usher them in. 'Let's get you fed.'

Fortune House, Saffi knew, hadn't always been a B&B. Trues had been there from the start; it still had that air of being a Victorian gentleman's residence. Visitors first arrived in a glassed-in porch area full of coats and boots. The B&B guests, if there were any, would leave theirs on special hooks to the side. Then came the hall with its ornate floral tiles and plaster mouldings. To the right was a stairwell carpeted in green, while on the left were two doors, one to the study and one to the dining room. At the far end were double doors to the living room and a corridor to the kitchen.

Dad put down their suitcases and kissed his mother on both cheeks, while Saffi and Milo stood awkwardly by. There was an earthy smell in the house like wet leaves. Then it was their turn, one after another, to be crushed against Grandma's grey cardigan, which smelled of mothballs, and have a kiss planted on their foreheads, which smelled of talcum powder. They had been with her a few months ago in London but she still fussed over them. Her eyes were bright as she helped Dad off with his coat. She was clearly glad to see them.

The same was not so evident of Grandad. 'Well,' said a gruff voice. 'What have we here.'

Saffi glanced up to find her grandfather standing in the living room doorway, frowning. Grandad's frown was impressive. He had huge eyebrows, at least three times as big as any ordinary person's. They were white aside from a few black hairs, and took up half of his forehead. He didn't come forward but waited there with his arms folded, glowering at Dad. He didn't fuss like Grandma.

'The prodigal returns,' he said.

'Hello, Father.'

Dad made no move to hug Grandad. Saffi waited as well, unsure. As to Milo, he had wandered off to look at the grandfather clock by the study door. Sir Henry True, Saffi recalled – the ancestor who built the house – also had some furnishings made. Grandad had told her all about it. The old clock with its illumined face was her favourite. The picture crescent above the numbers, a scene that was supposed to switch from day to night but remained stuck on night, showed a white castle by the sea, surmounted by stars. Apart from that, there were two chairs with clawed lion's feet and a mirror with a carved frame under the stairs. Milo had already moved on to inspect this last item.

'Leave it, Henry,' said Grandma, bustling past Grandad to the kitchen. 'They've had a long journey. Let's eat in peace.'

'They've et,' he growled after her. 'To avoid victuals here. Am I right, son?'

Without further warning, he strode forward and stuck out his arm at Dad. It was an instant before Saffi realised he was offering his hand in greeting. Dad shook it, as formal as if his father was a work colleague. Then it was her turn.

'You've grown since last I laid eyes on you, Tara Persephone.' Grandad pumped her arm up and down as he spoke. 'That's the spirit. No weaklings in our family.'

But when those eyebrows beetled in the direction of Milo, Saffi's heart sank. 'Won't shake hands with your old man?' he barked.

Milo looked smaller than ever, standing by the mirror. But he didn't miss a beat.

'I've been sick,' he answered, giving Grandad a smile of pure innocence. 'Hepatitis. You don't want to catch it.'

'Milo,' admonished Dad. 'Don't start.'

'No, no.' Grandad waved them both away. 'Leave him be. It's fine.'

'Grub's up,' Grandma called from the kitchen to Saffi's relief. 'Come and get it.'

The B&B kitchen at the back of the house was curiously cramped compared to the grand hall, as if it had been tacked on at the last minute by people who forgot they also needed to eat. There were red chequered curtains and a red chequered tablecloth. The yellow fridge hummed in its corner. Grandma cooked using a large, ungainly stove covered in blue enamel. Yet somehow, she managed to produce meals for her guests

13

here as well as the family suppers, such as they were. She was retrieving a dish that smelled of burnt sausage from the oven as they arrived.

Grub, Saffi decided as they sat down, was an appropriate word. Grandma had lived up to her reputation by cooking toad-in-the-hole. Saffi watched in some alarm as she dug through the pallid crust with a serving spoon, scooping up a ladleful of white paste and pink sausages for Dad.

'Just a little,' she said when it was her turn. The sausages came back smelling like Styrofoam in bacon sauce.

'I don't eat meat,' said Milo.

'He eats meat.' Dad handed over his son's plate. 'At least he did at lunch, when we stopped for burgers.'

'Careful. Those roadside places give you collywobbles,' said Grandma.

'Have you given thought to what we spoke of by phone?' Grandad turned to Dad, impatient with the subject of sausages.

'Maybe we should discuss that tomorrow.'

The way her father answered – in a low, dull voice, chewing methodically – made Saffi wonder what they were talking about. Dad wasn't his usual self. He hadn't made a single bad pun. Grandma meanwhile had her brows furrowed, mouth a round 'o' as if she wanted to speak. But Grandad got there first.

'We've run out of time,' he told Dad. 'They're coming.'

'You know I don't believe that.' Dad looked up sharply.

It sounded to Saffi as if Grandad expected guests at the

14

B&B, and Dad objected to them somehow. She doubted there was anyone in the upstairs suite right now, as there were no jackets hanging on the guest hooks.

'That's neither here nor there,' said Grandad.

Dad frowned. At that point, Milo held up his fork with a piece of pink sausage.

'Is this made of rubber?'

'Milo. Enough!'

Dad almost shouted it. Saffi stared at him in shock. She had rarely heard him use that tone, never about sausages. Whatever this business of the guests was, it made him lose patience.

Milo's cheeks blushed dark. 'I liked Mum's cooking,' he said. 'She made *tahdik*.'

There was a painful pause, before Grandma picked up the salad bowl, brandishing it like a trophy.

'Cherry toms, anyone?' she said. 'They may not be Persian, but they're from your grandad's garden.'

The conversation limped on from there. Milo didn't speak for the rest of the meal or eat the food on his plate, and no one made him. There was no more talk of guests. Afterwards, they rose and said goodnight to Grandad, who told them that he expected to see them all bright and early tomorrow, as there were no shirkers in the True family. Grandma led them to their rooms on the second floor while Dad followed behind with the suitcases.

One thing was sure, Saffi thought as she trudged after her grandmother. Trues didn't shirk family. Photos of the clan hung all the way up the stairwell, people both known and unknown to her: pictures of Dad as a child, of her grandparents young. There were some she had never met who were True legends, like Aunt Moira who ran away to America and Cousin Jimmy who swallowed a bee. Only a few of Mum, though it couldn't be for lack of room. From time to time, empty spaces and discoloured squares showed where a frame had been taken down.

That wasn't the only mystery in the house. On the first-floor landing was a green door in a pebbled glass partition. The corridor beyond led to the guest suite. The B&B rooms were strictly off limits to the children.

'Who was Grandad talking about at dinner?' Saffi asked Grandma as they passed by the door. 'Who's arriving?'

'Foreign guests.' Her grandmother answered shortly. 'They keep funny hours. Don't worry if you hear noise late at night, love.'

She didn't offer any details. Saffi didn't press her, though she was curious. What sort of foreign? Why funny hours? But Grandma was silent and preoccupied as she showed them to their rooms. The children would take one to the right of the stairs, while Dad had another down the hall. This was new. They had slept on cots together last time.

As it turned out, the room Saffi was to share with Milo was an improvement on anything in the London flat. The large square room under the eaves had wooden beds and a rag carpet of many colours. There were shelves containing books and magazines, as well as a model *Millennium Falcon*

Dad made when he was a boy. Even sharing, they had plenty of space to themselves. Once they dragged the suitcase inside and said goodnight to Grandma, Milo marched off to flop down on one of the beds with his arms splayed out. It was past his bedtime, so it was up to Saffi to open the suitcase, find his pyjamas and coax him into them. Milo was still flushed with anger from dinner as she pulled on his pyjama bottoms.

'I hate it here,' he complained. 'Why couldn't we stay in London?'

'Because Dad can't care for us on his own.' She bit her tongue so as not to mention the lying.

'I liked London. We had friends.'

'We'll make new ones.'

The answer was mostly to convince herself. Saffi felt a stab of pointless longing, then – for everything to be how it used to be. Home. London. Mum.

Milo scowled. 'Grandad's mean. They're both stupid. Grandma thinks Mum cooked curry. They don't know anything.'

'They're old, Milo. They don't get it.'

'The house is spooky. That mirror in the hall has eyes.'

'It does not.'

'Does, too. They followed me when I was looking at the clock.'

'That's it. I'm going to go brush my teeth. You can come if you like.'

But since her brother seemed determined to sulk, she left

him behind. Just as she was crossing the landing, Dad stepped out of his room.

'How's he doing?' he whispered, meaning Milo.

'Not great,' she answered.

'I'm sorry about dinner. Shouldn't have lost my temper.'

Saffi shrugged. 'He misses home.'

'Moving is hard.' Dad was nodding. 'It's an adjustment . . .'

'It's not that,' said Saffi. 'It's Mum.'

There was a look on Dad's face that might have been sadness. Or it might have been admiration. Something, in any case, wrestled there.

'You understand a lot,' he said.

He was talking to her as if she was a grown-up – as if she might advise him. Though when it came to Milo, no one really knew what to do. Least of all Dad.

'That's all I had to say.' He sighed, pointing to the bathroom. 'Want it first?'

Then he gathered her up in his arms and gave her a tight hug.

Later, when Saffi lay awake in bed in the dark, listening to her brother do his yoga breathing – inhale, hold then exhale, an exercise Mum had taught him long ago to help him relax – she racked her brains for ways to cheer him up. It struck her that it didn't have to be boring at the B&B, now she was older.

'How about we go to the beach tomorrow?' she said. 'We can use the cliff paths.'

He was quiet before answering. 'OK.'

'You can look for fossils. You'd like that, right?'

'Yes.'

After a longer pause, he spoke again. 'Saffi?'

'Yes?'

'I love you.'

'Love you, too.'

There was a further silence. At last, she heard the sleepy voice once more.

'It does have eyes, though.'

'Goodnight, Milo.'

Sometime in the middle of the night, Saffi woke with a start. The room was full of shifting shadows. It had been cloudy earlier but now a light shone through the window. The moon was up. The shadows were tree branches, shaken in the wind. There was a noise, too, but it wasn't the branches.

It was the sound of laughter on the stairs.

People were coming up from the front hall. She could hear voices, the light tread of many feet. The memory of guests filtered through her mind. So Dad was wrong and Grandad was right. They had come, whoever they were.

The laughter sent a shiver through Saffi. She got up and tiptoed out on the landing in her pyjamas. The lights were on so she had no trouble finding her way. She crept towards the edge of the stairwell, peering down.

'My Lady,' said someone from below.

Without thinking about it, Saffi moved down a green carpeted step, drawn by the sound of those voices. There was a musical quality to them, sweet and enchanting. She had never heard anyone speak like that – as if the speaker lived life only for the sake of pleasure and laughter, and all other experiences were unknown. These people sounded as if they had never been angry, or lost someone dear to them, or wept. Saffi longed to be like that. She moved down another step, then one more in growing confusion.

It seemed to her that there were too many steps. She could never reach the end of them. Her legs felt heavy, as if she was pushing through water. The stairwell stretched on and on like a dim green tunnel. She felt queasy and clutched at the banister.

Then, suddenly – as if an elastic had snapped back – she was at the bottom, facing the guest suite. She stopped in amazement. How had that happened? A few seconds ago, she couldn't walk down the flight. Yet here she was on the landing. The green door was open. Beyond it, she glimpsed figures, flashes of iridescent colour. Satin maybe, or feathers.

All at once, Grandma was there too, blocking her view. 'What are you doing, Saffi?' she hissed. 'Go back to bed!'

Saffi hurried up the stairs to her bedroom. But now, her curiosity was roused to fever pitch. Who were those guests? She lay in bed, listening intently, until she heard the sound of her grandparents creaking upstairs. They were talking in anxious murmurs, a strange contrast to the visitors' easy chatter.

'Answer by the seventh day,' she heard Grandad say before their bedroom door closed, and silence descended.

Who had to answer what? Saffi wondered. Across the room, Milo stirred in his sleep. She tossed and turned, questions gnawing at her. Why were her grandparents so worried? The guests had everyone in a flummox. She even speculated whether they were foreign royalty. Why else would one be called 'my Lady'?

She must have fallen asleep after that. When she opened her eyes, it was morning. Sunlight filtered through the curtains onto her bed.

3
Family

Milo was already awake, sitting on the floor in his triceratops pyjamas, surrounded by plastic dinosaurs. He hadn't wanted to box those toys up with their other things at the flat, and insisted on carrying them around in a small yellow backpack. He was deep in a game, murmuring over a brontosaurus and a T-rex like any seven-year-old. The normalcy of the scene took Saffi aback. She had a strong sense that she had missed something. Then, she remembered.

'Milo.' She sat up. 'I heard those guests last night. They're weird, all right.'

He gave her a thoughtful look. 'I dreamed of Mum. But she had green eyes.'

'I think they're royalty.' Saffi was still preoccupied by the guests as she reached for her rumpled jeans. 'Did you hear anything?'

Milo shook his head. 'Dad came in earlier, though. Message is: if you don't make it down by eight-thirty, you don't get any pancakes.'

'You might've said!' cried Saffi.

No wonder she felt she had missed something. Her watch read 8:25 a.m. She wriggled into her jeans and grabbed the nearest fresh T-shirt from the suitcase. She wanted those pancakes. It wasn't just that she was hungry. Dad always made pancakes before Mum got sick. This was a return to form.

'Come on,' she told Milo. 'You can wear your jammies.'

The green door to the guest suite was closed today as they passed it on their way downstairs, with Milo still in his pyjamas. In the hall, they had to pick a careful path across the tiles as someone had traipsed in puddles from outside. Meanwhile, a tantalising smell drifted through the doorway to the right of the grandfather clock. Dad was visible inside, seated at a long table.

The dining room at the B&B with its mahogany furniture, lily-of-the-valley wallpaper and sweeping vistas of the coast was usually reserved for visitors. But today, their father had set out breakfast there. The room opened out to a south-facing terrace, so sunlight streamed in, a welcome change from yesterday's grey. Dad sat reading his tablet. His plate was empty. But there were still pancakes on a platter, syrup and strawberries.

'I'd almost given up.' He smiled as they arrived. 'How d'you like my morning room? Your grandma doesn't want us here, but guests aren't down yet.'

So why was it a problem? Saffi puzzled over Grandma's reactions as she chose a seat between Dad and Milo. This was opposite the French windows; she piled pancakes on

Milo's plate with an eye on the view. It was glorious. Sunlight danced on the water far below. The darker parts of the sea were purple, the horizon wrapped in a golden haze. The True B&B perched on its clifftop could be gloomy on a winter's day. But today the bay was full of jewel-like colours.

Other treasures lay inside. Two cabinets to Saffi's right held a collection of ornaments belonging to the famous Sir Henry. On one shelf was a malachite mask on a stand, staring empty-eyed at the room. On another lay a carved elephant's tusk. Yet another held odd little grinning figurines with animal heads. Unlike Grandad, Dad didn't like to talk about family history; 'Empire swag', she remembered him calling that collection. But Saffi liked the ornaments. At Milo's age, she had been most impressed by a curved steel knife with a tiger's head hilt. She saw her brother ogling it now.

'Are there fossils in those cupboards?' he asked.

'How about a beach trip?' Dad didn't spare a glance at the cabinets. 'Then you can find your own.'

'I was going to take Milo by the cliff paths,' said Saffi.

'We can visit the one near town if you like.' Dad drummed the tablecloth with his fingers. 'I've some errands to run.'

Milo gave an enthusiastic cheer. Just then, Grandad entered the dining room, doing a double take when he saw the syrup-laden scene.

'Shouldn't have et in here,' he told Dad. 'Your mother's not impressed.'

'She'll be right.' Dad was unflappable. 'We'll be done soon, eh, kids?'

'We're going to look for fossils.' Milo spoke with his mouth full of pancake.

'Remember, back by four,' warned Grandad. 'After that, tide's too high.'

'I'm thinking we'll drive into town.' Dad checked his watch. 'Make a morning of it.'

'Stuff and nonsense.' Grandad's frown deepened. 'What's wrong with their legs? Let 'em go. We've business to discuss here.'

'We can easily walk—' Saffi began, but her father interrupted.

'No, Saffi. We'll go in a minute.' He rose from the table. 'Your grandad and I just need a quick chat.'

It was a challenge – even Saffi could see that. There was a charged feeling in the air. Grandad gestured towards the hall. 'Fine. Study's that way, son.'

'We can talk right here.' Dad held his eye. 'Whatever's worth saying can be said in front of the children.'

Saffi gave Milo a look, willing him to be quiet so she could listen. Dad and Grandad's quarrel had jumped up a notch. Her brother stuck out his tongue at her.

'Be serious,' Grandad snorted. 'They've arrived. If you'd go upstairs—'

But another voice from the hall cut him off. 'Heavens, what a mess. Look at these puddles! I'll have to mop up. Milo, you're not dressed yet.'

Grandma appeared in the doorway, wearing a large white apron with her sleeves rolled up. She looked put out, a smear of flour on one cheek.

'Guests'll want breakfast,' she scolded. 'No time for shenanigans!'

As if on cue, a silvery peal echoed from the kitchen. It was a servant's bell, Saffi realised, the sort people used to have in grand houses. She didn't recall seeing one there before. It was an oddly old-fashioned thing to have at the B&B. A spasm of panic crossed Grandma's face.

'What did I say? I'll thank you to clean up,' she threw over her shoulder at Dad, hurrying away.

'We're not done talking,' Grandad told his son. 'You've a duty, Will. We're all depending on you.'

He followed Grandma out. Dad sighed.

'Upstairs, you two.' He shooed the children away. 'Get dressed before your grandparents have a hissy fit.'

'But who—' Saffi meant to ask about the guests.

'Please, Saf,' Dad interrupted. 'If you want any chance of an outing, we need to make a start. And bring the day bag, would you?' he called as they trailed off towards the stairs. 'We'll have sandwiches.'

Saffi did as she was told, plodding up to the bedroom with bad grace. There, she let Milo dress alone and went to empty the dinosaur bag. She wanted to be back downstairs as soon as possible. But Milo dawdled.

'There wasn't a bell in the kitchen,' he objected. 'We'd have seen it.'

'I guess we didn't notice.' Saffi dumped velociraptors on the bed.

'I'd have seen,' he said, stubborn. 'And those eyes are back in the mirror. I saw them.'

Saffi let the lie slide, more concerned by Dad and Grandad. But when she left her brother with a warning to hurry up and returned to the dining room, she found it deserted. Thinking that Dad might have made a start on the sandwiches, she continued on to the kitchen, where silvery bell notes echoed out.

A cloud of steam engulfed her as she opened the door, accompanied by a clattering noise. Her grandparents were in the throes of making several English breakfasts with all the trimmings. Eggs fried on a griddle, bacon sizzled, kettles boiled. Grandma retrieved a dish of brown sausages from her oven, while Grandad stacked trays with teapots and the best china. Homemade tarts and scones in various states of preparation sat on the counter. There was enough food for an army. Dad was nowhere to be seen.

'Breakfast rush, love,' Grandma called over the din. 'Don't mind us.'

All this while, the bell notes rang on, an endless jingle-jangle though surely the guests had made their point. Saffi glanced up to see in surprise that a silver bell was mounted on a bracket above the kitchen table, attached to a rope stretching through a hole in the ceiling. Milo was right. They should have noticed it.

'Coming through.'

Grandad's comment roused her as she stood blinking at the ceiling. He was waiting with a tray. When Saffi stepped back, he strode out of the door.

'Is that bell new?' she asked Grandma.

'What, love?' Her grandmother set more plates of food out on trays. 'Can't talk. Could you be a darling and put those tarts in the pantry? There, on the table.'

Without waiting for an answer, she hurried out of the kitchen, carrying a tray loaded with eggs, bacon and toast. The bell carried on ringing in a demented way. A minute later, Grandad returned for the final tray. When he was gone, the summons ceased, leaving Saffi in ringing silence. She shook her head and went to retrieve Grandma's jam tarts.

That was when she heard the voice. 'True child,' someone said.

The words were low but clear. All the hairs on Saffi's arms stood on end. She looked about her at the deserted kitchen. The voice had been husky, somehow close to the ground. No one was about. Having decided that her mind was playing tricks on her, she picked up the box of tarts and carried it to the pantry.

But there she halted again, this time in amazement. The pantry was full, bursting with every dainty and delicacy imaginable. Last night, it had been half-empty. Her grandparents stocked ordinary things like pickles, crackers, sardines, flour. Now, the shelves groaned with food. Instead of sardines, there was a platter of sole – instead of crackers, colourful French *macarons*. Pickles were replaced by pâté.

One of the jokes Mum used to make when they visited Grandma and Grandad was that all the money in the world couldn't give them a taste for fine dining. But this fare might have graced the table of a king.

At that moment, Saffi heard it again: a low, rasping laugh. She dumped the tarts on a shelf and backed out, heart racing, only to jump with surprise when someone knocked on the kitchen door.

A shadow loomed behind the glass. Saffi stared at it, spooked. The shadow sighed with impatience. When she finally opened up, she saw a blonde woman in high heels and a smart beige skirt suit, a bottle of champagne under one arm. She was such an unexpected vision on the back doorstep that Saffi assumed she was lost.

'Can I help you?' she asked.

'You must be one of the True children.' The woman showed a perfect set of white teeth. 'How lovely. Is your father home?'

'Why?' asked Saffi. It was perhaps rude. Her nerves were rattled.

'Oh dear.' The woman laughed. 'I've been remiss, not introduced myself. I'm Lily Jackson. From up the road.' She gave her bottle a merry jiggle. 'I used to go to school with your dad. I've brought him a welcome home gift.'

The last thing Saffi wanted to do right now was talk to someone who had known Dad long ago, before she and Milo were born. Before Mum. She reached out to take the bottle, summoning up her crispest London voice.

'He's busy right now, but I'll give it to him. Thank you so much.'

Usually, the voice was enough to shut anyone down. But this Lily was made of firmer, or in any case more inquisitive, stuff.

'Is he that busy?' She peered over Saffi's shoulder. 'I could just pop in . . .'

'He went to town,' lied Saffi.

Dad's car stood in the driveway. Lily would have passed it on her way here. She gave Saffi a doubtful look. But nothing cracked her polish.

'What a shame,' she said. 'I wanted to say. If he needs anything – even a little babysitting – I'm here. Do give him the message. Lovely to meet you.'

With that, she turned and tripped away across the gravel. Saffi watched her until she got into what had to be her own car – a brand new silver Mini – thinking, *babysitting?* After that, she closed the door and deposited the bottle on the table, where she almost collided with her grandmother.

'Watch where you're going, love.' Grandma looked flustered, her grey curls unravelling. Then she noticed the champagne.

'Good grief, what's this,' she said.

Saffi took a deep breath. She was being silly. There had been no laugh while she stood in the pantry, no voice earlier on, nothing unusual. This was an old house. It must have been air in the pipes, an echo in the drains.

'From a lady called Lily Jackson,' she told Grandma. 'For Dad.'

'Oh, Lily.'

Grandma rolled her eyes, turning to her kitchen cupboards. She had no great opinion of Lily, apparently. Saffi began to relax. But she hadn't imagined that food.

'I was going to make sandwiches.' She followed her grandmother. 'Can I use the pâté?'

'Ah.' Grandma looked apologetic. 'I should've said. That food is only for guests, love. You'll find bread and cheese in fridge.'

Of course it was for the guests. Grandma and Grandad had probably ordered it in. Saffi didn't know why she was so jumpy this morning.

'Dad says he'll take us out for the day,' she went on.

'Oh, I doubt he'll have time for that.' Grandma was rummaging inside one of the upper cupboards for flour and sultanas. She didn't turn around.

'Why not?' asked Saffi.

The answer came from within the cupboard. 'This business with your grandad. Signing over ownership of the B&B, all that paperwork. So much to do . . .'

'The B&B?'

Saffi frowned. When Dad talked to them about staying with Grandma and Grandad, he made it sound temporary. He was a historian who taught at a school and wrote scholarly books with titles like *Doggerland: A Drowned History*, which Saffi didn't read. She couldn't imagine him running a B&B, changing sheets and answering bells.

'Well, that's what your grandad wants.' Grandma darted her a wry look, half-moon glasses slipping. 'Your dad has other ideas.'

At last, Saffi thought she understood. Grandad wanted Dad to take over the B&B, but her father wasn't keen. No wonder he was so eager to leave. That reminded her of Milo, who was taking ages to get dressed. She strode out to the hall, irritated.

But there, she paused again. It wasn't for any special reason. Milo was already downstairs, standing in his socks by the mirror, trainers in hand. Saffi could hear Dad and Grandad arguing in the study, their voices muffled by the door. Her brother was absorbed by something in the mirror. For a second, she thought he was admiring himself. He stretched out his hand to touch the glass.

'What's up?' she asked, walking over.

He glanced at her before turning back. Then, his face fell. Saffi couldn't see why. The mirror looked the same, its carved frame an echo of the leaf motif on the clock. Stuck at the base was a smear of sand from someone's boot.

'Nothing,' he said.

That was a lie, thought Saffi. He was blushing.

In the study, Grandad's voice grew louder. 'Bad idea,' he said. 'She'll take offence.'

Who was *she*? Saffi wondered. Everyone was on edge this morning. Her dad and grandad didn't seem to be talking about the B&B at all. She was about to go and knock on the door, when something else happened. She had the impression, just for an instant, of a face staring out of the mirror.

Those features, wrenchingly familiar. That curly dark hair. Mum's face.

'Did you see it, too?' Milo had an eager look.

Saffi's heart beat fast, as it had in the kitchen. She told herself to calm down. It had been a trick of the light, her own reflection doubled up. Even the colours were wrong. The face in the mirror was darker than Mum's, the eyes light as ice. Milo must have had the same experience. Before she could ask, however, the study door opened to show Dad.

'You can't expect me to believe this nonsense,' he said.

Grandad arrived behind. 'Not "nonsense",' he insisted. 'Every generation chooses: it's our legacy. Why not take pride in it?'

'Are we leaving, Dad?' Saffi asked. She didn't want any more arguments.

Her father didn't look at her. 'Maybe you shouldn't take so much pride,' he told Grandad. 'Maybe that's the problem.'

'At least I know who I am.'

'A stubborn old man, clinging to the past?'

Dad was trying to joke but Grandad glared. 'Anoush knew,' he said.

Anoush was Mum's name. Dad's expression grew hard.

'That's low,' he said. 'Bringing her into it.'

'What did Mum know?' Milo asked in his fluting voice.

'Dad?' Saffi tried to catch his eye, anxious. 'What's going on?'

'Nothing.' Dad frowned. 'Your grandad's not thinking straight. Are you, Father?'

Grandad said nothing. Dad strode to the front door with a face like a cloud. The guests, Saffi noticed distractedly, had left no coats.

'I'm late. Got to go.' Dad was avoiding them, talking the way he did when he wanted to be alone. 'Sorry, kids. No time for our beach outing. Maybe tomorrow? Saf, do you mind taking Milo, like you said? Don't forget tide tables. Come home by top paths, it's safer.'

He stepped outside, leaving the door open. Whatever the trouble with Grandad was, the mention of Mum had been too much for him. It reminded Saffi of the bad times last year. She watched him stride away across the drive.

'Will.' Grandad hurried after. 'You can't ignore it. We'll lose everything.'

'Speaking of which,' Dad's voice drifted back, 'you'd do well to drop that land purchase of yours. Man has a son. It's not fair.'

'Fair's nowt to do with it,' Grandad huffed and puffed. 'That's just business.'

The two of them began arguing with renewed energy on the way to the car, this time about someone's mismanaged holiday park and Grandad's plan to buy it. Neither spoke of Mum again. As their voices faded away, the grandfather clock gave a hiccupping little whir and struck ten silver chimes. Saffi checked her watch. The clock was five minutes fast.

'Know what?' said Milo. 'I think they're scared. That's why they argue so much.'

'Maybe.'

Saffi was still trying to make sense of what she had heard. Outside, Dad started up the car and drove away, a scrape of wheels on gravel.

'They're scared of those guests,' said Milo.

It was the sort of comment an older child might make. She glanced at him, curious. He was standing by the mirror, tracing his finger on the oak leaf designs.

'So scared,' he continued, 'they don't notice what's happening.'

'What d'you mean?'

'I mean,' said Milo slowly, 'the changes. The whole house is changing. And no one says a thing about it.'

4
Secrets

'What do you mean, changes?' Saffi stared at Milo.

In addition to being a clever child interested in dinosaurs and fossils, her brother had an imaginative streak. Sometimes, it was hard to tell if he set out to lie or if he truly believed what he was saying. There was the hepatitis kind of lie, or the eyes kind. Then there was this. Something in his tone made her listen. He meant it.

'What I say. Stuff is different.' He patted the mirror frame. 'See this carving? Yesterday, acorns were in the corners. Today, they've moved round so there's spaces in the corners.'

Saffi came to inspect it. 'It's the same mirror,' she said after a moment.

Then, she remembered the fleeting image of a face. She, too, had been seeing and hearing things all morning. Not that that proved anything.

'I didn't say they'd switched the mirror.' Milo pointed. 'It's the carving.'

Saffi thought of what the grief counsellor would say, in

his brown office in Wandsworth. Everyone else in the family had secrets. So Milo had decided to invent some of his own. Carvings didn't change.

'Come on,' her brother wheedled. 'You must have seen something. Check out the wallpaper! Yesterday it was green, today it's yellow . . .'

The pattern on the hall wallpaper with its lilies and stems was the same, Saffi was certain. True, the place looked lighter, but that might be due to the sunlight.

'I get it,' she said. 'We're in a new place, it's weird. I feel the same. I bet Dad does, too. But it's you, not the mirror.'

Milo waved her explanation away. 'I'm serious!' he protested. 'If you'd stop being a big sister and believe me . . .'

Saffi closed her eyes. 'Milo. No more stories. There's too much else going on.'

'That's when it changes. When we're too busy to look.'

She was sick of arguing with him. 'Whatever,' she snapped. 'If you want the beach, we'd best get on.'

She moved off towards the kitchen to make sandwiches. He followed, glum.

'You're not looking,' he grumbled. 'Only thing that's the same is the clock.'

They happened to be walking by it. Saffi glanced up at the images on the number wheel: a boy in a white tunic, a swan, a lion, a whale. Above them was the castle scene. There was a line of text under it, just visible. *And there was no more sea.* Her brother didn't need to invent stories. The house and its contents were curious enough.

For now, Saffi hoped an outing would distract him – though he started complaining again while she prepared their packed lunch, this time about the food. She might have guessed that cheese sandwiches and apples wouldn't please him. As soon as he saw the pantry fare, he clamoured for pâté and *macarons*, and was disappointed when Grandma said he couldn't have them. To console himself, he began what Saffi suspected was a search for magical changes, standing on a chair to stare at the bell. He did it for so long that Grandma asked if he was looking for dust.

Saffi was quite happy with bread and cheese. It was quantity rather than quality she was after, anyway. She wanted to walk along the beach to Breakwell, a journey of about an hour. The town was small enough that she thought she might run into Birdy again. Despite their shaky start, she felt a need to talk to someone. Anyone. Besides, she didn't like how they had left things yesterday. While she hadn't yet suggested it to Milo, she was sure he wouldn't turn down an opportunity to go beachcombing.

After sandwiches, the next job was to look up tide tables in the study. Dad or Grandad must have been using the computer, for she found the desk covered in printouts she had to sweep aside to access the keyboard. She glanced at them as the printer chugged to life. They were old records, a log for a vessel named the *White Hind*, listing cargo transported for the Honourable Company. The captain was one John Henry True.

What's *coolies*, she wondered idly.

She didn't read on, as the printer spat its pages on the floor. These showed high tide at six, which meant they had six hours to wander safely on the beach. Pages in hand, she went to join Milo in the hall. Grandma had begun to vacuum the dining room in the meantime: a steady whine rose from behind the closed door. Milo watched as Saffi threw on her hoodie, then checked the contents of the bag. He had a nonchalant air, thumbs hooked in his jeans.

'So,' he said. 'I guess you didn't see them.'

'See?' Saffi pulled the drawstring shut, half-listening.

'The photos by the stairs.'

It was his changes game again. 'Enough, Milo!' Saffi cried. 'I'm sick of your—'

Then, she broke off. She had thrown an exasperated glance at the stairwell, only to find that there were no empty spaces between the frames. They marched on in an unbroken line.

'So you do see,' Milo said, exultant, in the silence that followed.

Saffi walked over to look. As far as she could tell, the photos were old ones, prints faded to orange. Some showed a young Dad with more hair than now, or long-dead members of the True clan. Was that Aunt Moira as a young girl, before her America adventure, blonde-haired and pretty? Other pictures made Saffi's heart skip a beat.

'That's Mum,' she breathed.

'A lot of them are Mum,' said Milo.

Saffi climbed another step. There was that dear familiar

face again – but round, smiling, shockingly young. Mum was in her early twenties. That was when she had met Dad. The pictures were all taken at Fortune House. As Saffi gazed at them, the vacuum noise ceased in the dining room. Her grandmother emerged, dragging her red machine.

'Grandma?' called Saffi from the stairwell.

'What is it, love?' Grandma paused.

'Did you put the missing pictures back?'

'It wasn't her,' said Milo.

Grandma left the vacuum to come to the foot of the stairs, staring up in puzzlement. Then she gave a cry of dismay, pushing past Saffi to unhook first one, then another picture from the wall. Milo's face had an *I told you so* look.

'If this is someone's hare-brained joke . . .'

Grandma fumed as she climbed up the steps. Every so often, she would stop and unhook a photograph, placing it under her arm.

'Why are you taking them down?' asked Saffi. 'We like seeing Mum.'

Her grandmother had a flustered air. 'I'm sorry, love. We've got lots of family ones, as you know. But these are older. Your dad doesn't like being reminded, and I respect that. If this was your grandad, I'll have words with him.'

Now that she said it, Saffi had a flash of memory – this time from the London flat after the funeral. Dad, packing up boxes of old photo albums from before Saffi was born. *I can't look at them anymore, Saf.* So he had done the same thing at home. It was odd of Grandad to put them back.

'It wasn't Grandad,' Milo said, after Grandma had gone. 'It was ghosts. This place is haunted.'

'No way, Milo—'

'You saw her in the mirror.' He cut her short. 'Don't say you didn't.'

Her. The word made Saffi hesitate. So he had seen a woman's face in the mirror, not a doubled-up reflection of himself. That was upsetting in a way she couldn't define. She had no explanation for it.

After that, she was desperate to leave the house. Her thoughts were in a whirl as she pulled on her trainers. The business of the photographs was spooky enough without ghosts, as if an intruder had crept into the hall to play a trick on them. Even if this was part of Dad and Grandad's undeclared war, it felt exaggerated. Things had gone too far.

It was past ten-thirty by the time they left by the back garden, making for the cliff stairs. Luckily, the weather was perfect, sunny but not too warm. Clouds raced through blue skies while the wind stirred the branches of the trees. Halfway down the slope, they stopped to wave goodbye to Grandma on the terrace. From this angle, the B&B looked like a sad face to Saffi, its white walls wan beneath a peaked roof. Instead of mouths, the windows resembled glassy eyes.

'She knows the score.' Milo kept his eye on Grandma. 'She's scared.'

'It's got to be a gang,' whispered Saffi. 'Maybe Grandad's in debt for all that food. The pictures are some sort of threat.'

She had come up with this theory after careful consideration. Milo shrugged.

'Grandad's got money,' he said. 'He's buying land.'

He was right. But Saffi wasn't ready for his explanation. 'I can't believe in ghosts and stuff without proof.'

'It's not that you can't,' he answered, resigned. 'You won't.'

He turned and walked on towards the cliffs. Grandma had gone back inside. Saffi was about to follow her brother, when something else caught her attention.

Someone, a stranger, was watching them from the house. A woman stood at an upstairs window – one of the full-length ones in the guest suite, with a Juliet balcony. How long she had been there, Saffi didn't know. Dressed all in white, she resembled a saint in stained glass with her halo of golden curls. Even at this distance, Saffi could tell that she was beautiful. Her gaze, keen and bright, was fixed on them.

It looked almost hungry.

The vision lasted just long enough for her to be sure it was real, after which the woman disappeared. Was this *my Lady?* Saffi shuddered. The feeling of being watched persisted as she hurried away, doubly glad to have left the house behind. She decided not to tell Milo what she had seen, not yet. It would only confirm his haunted theory. The wind hit her face as she caught up with him on the clifftop; in front of them was a wooden rail covered in chicken wire, then a hundred-foot drop. Glancing over it, she saw three flights of wooden stairs zigzagging down a slope of scree. Beyond that was the smoky blue bay.

Though the cliffs were at their lowest point for miles, it was still a tumble to the beach. Saffi started down the first flight ahead of Milo, cautioning him to hold on to the railing. Restless gulls flew above. Once, when they were both small, Dad had taken them up to Bempton Cliffs to see the seabird colonies. Saffi had a memory of clouds of white and grey rising up, more like weather than birds: terns, kittiwakes, puffins with red beaks. Here, only the raucous herring gulls circled. The air was sharp with a seaweed tang.

'So. You want proof.' Her brother stomped after her. 'How do we get it?'

'I'd like to go into town again,' she said, trying to put the figure at the window out of her mind. 'Find Birdy. He might help us.'

They had reached the bottom of the stairs, where a series of ramps led to the shore. Milo was silent for a moment. His answer when it came was muffled by wind.

'He won't.'

'How do you know?'

'He didn't like us before. He won't change.'

Saffi hoped he was wrong. At the end of the ramp, they stepped onto piled pebbles at the base of the cliffs, breathing in the salt smell. The horseshoe-shaped beach below the B&B was sheltered and empty, its white stones laced with seaweed. The only noise was the crunch of their feet and the hiss of the tide. She paused to watch the waves rise and spend themselves, one after another. The motion was hypnotic.

'Talking to Birdy won't prove it.' Milo was still vexed about his ghosts.

'Got a better idea, genius?'

He didn't answer. He wasn't watching the waves but staring at the wet sand near the water with a concentrated look.

'Listen,' he said. 'D'you hear that?'

And then, because the bluffs cut them off from strong winds, she did. A sound carried towards them, faint but unmistakeable. It wasn't just waves or seagulls crying. At first, Saffi thought it might be wind blowing through rocks. Soon, however, she realised it was something else.

At times mournful, at times merry, rippling along with gusto before beginning again in a minor key, a tune drifted on the breeze.

Someone was playing a flute on the far side of the bay.

5

Friends

The cliffs at Flamborough Head were the oldest chalk deposits in the north, at least according to Dad. Some of the rocks were a hundred million years old. Geology enthusiasts came to see the caves and stacks on the north side of the peninsula, or the fossils to the south. If he had been interested in finding ancient sponges today, Milo might have been lucky. As it was, he scrambled after Saffi along the stony beach, intent on another discovery.

At the end of the bay, they could hear the flute plainly. It played a strange tune, half-happy and half-sad, and kept stopping and starting. The rocky strand was narrow and full of seaweed on the point, underwater only a few hours ago. Saffi found herself hurrying Milo past the last bluffs. After that, they were able to see down the next bay, which was longer and shallower than the one below the B&B. The cliffs marched to the east in tiers of white and green.

They were getting close to the flute player now. Saffi cautioned Milo with a finger to her lips as they passed a final boulder. A moment later, she caught sight of a blond head.

It was Birdy. He sat about twenty feet away on a flat rock, playing a wooden flute or pipe. It was oddly unsurprising to see him there, as if he belonged on this beach by the smoky sea; she remembered what he told them about his dad's holiday park. He must live nearby. The challenge would be not to frighten him off. It was like approaching a shy wild animal.

'Let me talk to him first,' she whispered to Milo.

Her brother made a face. 'Fine by me.'

Saffi chose not to creep up on their quarry, but stepped out in the open. 'Hey,' she called. 'Birdy.'

He stopped playing to glance round, but didn't seem either pleased or displeased to see them. 'Ey up,' he answered.

'Heard you playing,' Saffi said, though this was obvious.

He got up and walked towards her, sliding the wooden instrument into a pocket in the lining of his jacket. He was still wearing the trainers with green laces. A few feet away he stopped, the wind tugging his hair.

'I come here to practise because it's empty.'

Saffi couldn't tell if he meant that he would rather they went. 'You left in a hurry yesterday,' she said.

It came out sounding more like an accusation than she intended. He squinted at her in the sunlight.

'Didn't think you'd want to hang around likes of me.'

'That's not true. Sorry if I sounded rude.'

'Aye.'

There was another awkward pause. His way of surveying her with an ironic half-smile made Saffi want to leave again.

'Look,' she said. 'We're new here. We don't know anyone. Right now, we could do with a friend . . .'

His eyebrows shot up. 'You want to be friends? With me?'

By this point, Milo couldn't contain himself. 'None of this is important,' he burst out. 'The B&B's haunted. There's poltergeists. Paranormal phenomena.'

'Para-what now?' Birdy was taken aback.

'What he means,' Saffi said, 'is that weird things keep happening. I was hoping we'd run into you. Maybe you can help us . . .'

But she stopped there, because Birdy's face was full of astonishment, as if her plea for help was stranger than any ghost.

'You really don't know, do you,' he said.

'Know what?' Saffi wondered what she was missing.

He gave no further explanation. Instead, he turned to Milo.

'What's this haunting, then?'

'Stuff changes. Wallpaper. Furniture.' Milo's answer was eager. 'Pictures, too. Saffi can't see it but I do. And there's a bell that rings and rings . . .'

'I did see the pictures,' Saffi put in. 'Some old photographs that were taken down. No one knows who hung them back.'

'And food.' Milo had evidently forgotten his claim that Birdy wouldn't help, jumping from foot to foot with excitement. 'The pantry's full of amazing food.'

'Woah.' Birdy held out his hands for calm.

He looked from one to the other, as if he doubted they

were serious. 'Let's walk and talk,' he said at last. 'Stay away from cliff's edge. There's rockslides.'

And that was that. The three of them set off with the cliffs to their left. While Milo launched into an account of his changes theory, Saffi found herself marvelling at the unexpected ease of it all. She had wanted to find Birdy, and here he was. He hadn't wanted to talk yesterday, but now he did. It was like magic. She had someone to confide in. The beach was as empty as he had promised, a strip of smooth, egg-shaped stones about a quarter of a mile long. Apart from gulls and a black cormorant, they had it to themselves. Birdy listened with close attention to Milo's rather wandering tale as they crunched over the pebbles. He only spoke at the very end.

'And you think it's haunted?' he asked Saffi.

'I'm not sure,' she said. It was strange to even be considering it. 'The pictures could be a prank, or a threat . . . the bell was weird, granted. I told Milo there might be other explanations. The guests, for one.'

'Guests?' He darted her a quick look.

'They arrived in the night. I don't know who they are,' said Saffi. 'Except . . . they might be lords and ladies from the way they talk.'

'Ah.'

Birdy's tone was non-committal. Saffi realised how silly it all sounded, taken together: royal guests, changing wallpaper, extra bells.

'Feels like someone messing with us,' she said. 'Could be anyone.'

'It's ghosts.' Milo huffed with impatience.

But Birdy looked as if he had remembered something, and was unsure whether to mention it. He dug his hands further in his pockets as he walked.

'What?' prompted Saffi.

'Old tales.' He gave a sheepish grin. 'Stuff changing round at home means the Fair Folk are angry.'

'Ghosts,' Milo insisted. 'Not fairies.'

Birdy didn't argue. But Saffi saw the look on his face. There was more.

'D'you know any other stories about Fortune House?' she pressed. 'I don't mean ghosts.'

'What kind of stories?' He was cautious again.

'I think maybe Grandad's involved in shady stuff. No, Milo,' she said as her brother started to object. 'You heard them talking about someone who wanted to meet Dad.'

Birdy was silent, trudging along with his shoulders hunched. 'I don't know about that,' he replied at last. 'But my dad says Mr True'll do anything for money. Bear in mind he hates your family, so.'

Saffi caught his eye. 'Why?'

Birdy's face had gone pink. 'Well. You'll know soon enough. We're going out of business. Dad'll have to sell up. Your grandad might buy park.'

'Oh,' Saffi said.

Then, she stopped on the stony beach, remembering Grandad's words by the door. 'It's *your* home he's buying,' she said with dismay. 'I'm sorry, Birdy. I didn't know.'

Birdy nodded. He didn't talk about it as they continued on, though Saffi guessed he hadn't said everything. Maybe he was being careful in front of Milo. She resolved to ask him again, in private. Right now, it was his turn to be curious.

'So,' he said. 'Your dad's a True. What about your mum?'

Saffi remembered, looking at his pleasant, inquisitive face, that they didn't know the first thing about each other. He had no idea Mum had died. Milo was skipping ahead. She lowered her voice.

'Iranian. She came here when she was small,' she added, because Birdy looked so astonished and delighted. 'I don't know that side of the family.'

He was about to ask another question, when Milo called to them. 'Can we go on to the next beach, Saf?' he wheedled. 'Please?'

She realised they were approaching the end of the bay. Ahead of them lay another bluff, where a shelf of brown rocks sent long fingers into the sea. Before she could answer, Birdy spoke.

'You wanted smuggler's caves. If you don't have to be home for lunch, there's a good one by that bluff.'

'Please, Saf.' Milo almost danced with glee. 'Birdy can have my sandwich.'

'There's plenty for all,' she laughed.

'Great.' Birdy beckoned. 'Step where I do. Careful of seaweed, it slides.'

They followed, scrambling over the brown rocks. These were reef-like, broken by lines and troughs filled with water and purplish seaweed, so the going was tricky. It looked to Saffi as if some huge mythical beast had scored the beach with its claws. The surf was a far-off line. Halfway to the point, surrounded by sharp rocks, she had a sudden doubt. It would be terrifying if that white line rushed in. But when she checked her watch, she saw that it was twelve-thirty. The tide was at its lowest point. Birdy was right. It was safe.

'They used these caves for contraband, back in the day,' he was saying as they picked their way across the seaweed. 'Cognac, brandy, the like. They'd hide cargo in coffins, lower 'em overboard as if there'd been a death. Afterwards, when customs inspectors were gone, they'd haul 'em up again.'

Saffi was impressed. Birdy came alive when he talked about the smuggling. He even took his hands out of his pockets to act out the coffin bit.

'How come you know so much about it?' she asked.

She had to raise her voice, as it was windy on the exposed rocks. They had also fallen behind as Milo was struggling. When Birdy saw that, he stopped to wait.

'Lived here all my life,' he said when they caught up. 'White Lady caravan park, by Beacon Hill.' He pointed to the cliffs. 'There's loads of history here – both nice and not.'

'How long till we reach your cave?' Saffi's gaze was on the far-off waves.

Birdy smiled, guessing the reason for her anxiety. 'Don't fret about tides. If this were North Landing, we'd be underwater in two ticks. Bad beaches up there. This one's fine, though. Entrance is just behind that rock.'

He indicated a chalk outcrop. It wasn't far. Even Milo picked up his pace, lured on by the promise of the cave. Once they were past the bluff, the view opened out to the next cove. After that was a large sandy beach, larger than any Saffi had seen since Breakwell. It was also more frequented, with fishing boats drawn up to the shingle and faraway bathers. She saw no sign of a cave when Birdy came to a halt.

'Where is it?' she asked.

Even as she spoke, she was distracted by a sound like a whistle. She thought Birdy was playing his flute again and turned to look. He stood smiling by the cliff's foot, hands in pockets, wind whipping his hair. From this angle, she could make out a dark space in the rock beside him. The outcrop was separated from the rest by a fissure, invisible unless you knew where to look. A grown man might fit in sideways. When the wind rose, it made a sighing, whistling sound in the gap.

'Hear that?' said Birdy. 'Means we're safe. Breeze swings with the tide.'

Of course, he was smug about the cave – and Saffi was entranced, as was Milo. He leaped towards the opening with a shout of delight.

'Hold on,' Birdy cautioned. 'I'll go first.'

He slid through the entrance ahead of them, turning his body so he wouldn't brush the crumbling rocks. Saffi and Milo followed suit. Within, the fissure was wider and floored with pebbles. A blowhole formed a chimney open to the sky. To their right was the entrance to the cave proper.

'No tourists here.' Birdy had a wicked grin as he ducked through. 'We don't tell 'em.'

The space inside was larger than Saffi expected, about ten feet wide and twice as long. There must have been fissures overhead because sunlight filtered in, enough to see by. The pale walls glistened so it would be at least partly flooded at high tide. She could just imagine generations of Lythes stashing barrels in the dry corners.

'Can we eat lunch here?' asked Milo. His voice echoed.

'Depends how quick tides come in.' Saffi waited for Birdy's answer.

'So long as we don't dawdle,' he said.

They found a good place on a ledge near the back, and made quick work of the squashed sandwiches in Saffi's bag. Birdy accepted his with gratitude. Afterwards, he and Saffi stayed on the ledge while Milo made a tour of the cave. From outside came the far-off roar of the sea. The breeze made its mournful sound.

'Can I see that flute of yours?' Saffi asked.

He retrieved it with shy pride, placing it carefully in her hand. When she turned it over, she saw that it was very old, made of wood so dark that it was almost black. Along one side were leaf carvings that reminded her of the furniture at the B&B.

'That's beautiful,' she said. 'Where d'you get it?'

'A present,' he replied.

'And you've played like that, really well, all your life?'

'Started when I got it.'

He kept one eye on the flute: it was clearly a prized possession. He looked relieved when she handed it back. Saffi made sure Milo was far away before asking her next question.

'Right. What's this story between my grandad and your family?'

Birdy made a face. 'Park's not doing well. If Dad can't make payments to bank, we lose everything. House and land. Then Mr True buys it.'

'Why's that bad?' Saffi tried to follow the logic.

'Because,' answered Birdy, 'he gets it cheap, from bank. Nowt left for us. There's a saying about these parts: *deal with a True, come out blue.*'

Saffi remembered her grandad's comment about fairness and business with some discomfort. 'And if you lose the house?' she asked. 'Where d'you go?'

'Flat in town, probably.'

He sounded glum. Saffi's heart went out to him.

'Maybe my dad can change his mind,' she said. 'He wasn't keen on the plan.'

'Makes no difference.' Birdy sighed. 'If Mr True won't buy, others will.'

The dim crash of waves continued outside. Milo, Saffi saw, had reached the far end of the cave. He was in a happy dream, humming as he inspected the walls for fossils. This was her chance to talk frankly to Birdy.

'I know you know more about my family.' She dropped her voice to a whisper. 'Something's going on at the B&B. Am I right?'

That made him embarrassed. He glanced towards the door of the cave, as if he was worried someone might come in and hear them.

'Just old tales. You'll say it's daft.'

'Try me.'

Birdy looked unsure. She waited patiently until he spoke again. 'Fine. It's about that ancestor of yours, Sir Henry. Greedy so-and-so by all accounts.'

'My dad thinks the same,' Saffi said. 'But what's he got to do with us?'

'Sir Henry didn't start off loaded.' Birdy shrugged. 'One day, he's got nothing to his name – the next, he's captain of his own ship. Off he goes to India to make his fortune. Rumour is, he did a bad thing to get it.'

That wasn't all, Saffi could tell. Birdy stopped again. His ears had gone pink.

'Come on,' she groaned. 'What did he do?'

'All right, all right. He made a deal with the Fair Folk.'

'Fairies?'

Whatever Saffi was expecting, it wasn't this. She searched Birdy's face but he was apparently serious.

'For that ship,' he said. 'Also, Fortune House. Furniture and everything. All made by fairy craftsmen. There's magic in bricks of that place.'

'Are you trying to say . . . ?' She balked at the sheer

madness of it. 'You mean everything we've seen so far at the house is . . . ?'

'Magic.' He gave his half-smile. 'Look, I don't know. That's the tale.'

'You can't believe it?' Saffi was amazed. 'Fairies? Flitty things with wings?'

'It's what people say. No wings, though.'

He grinned again, as if admitting the joke. But it was Saffi who had a doubt, now. Was it possible? Could there be magic at Fortune House?

'Anyway,' Birdy went on, 'fairy deals are right ones for having strings attached. Since then, no True heir leaves Breakwell. Except your dad,' he amended. 'Why'd he go, if you don't mind me asking?'

'Mum preferred London.' Saffi thought this over. 'She said for work, but now . . . I'm not sure. Maybe she didn't get on with Grandad.'

She hadn't heard it put that way. But she did remember the reserve she sensed in Mum whenever they visited, the way she would purse her lips when Grandad talked about 'legacies' as he had that morning. There was something else, too – a feeling she had as a young child and didn't know how to put into words.

Mum was afraid. But not of Grandad.

Saffi shivered. It had grown suddenly cold in the cave.

'She wasn't far wrong,' said Birdy.

But he was glancing about him now, looking for Milo.

Her brother had stepped behind an outcrop of rock. He shouldn't be wandering off, Saffi realised.

'Milo,' she called. 'Stay where we can see you.'

Milo popped his head around the outcrop. 'I'm not a little kid anymore,' he said with irritation. 'I think I've found belemnite.'

He used the fancy word to fend them off. It worked. Birdy winced. 'I've no clue what that is,' he whispered to Saffi.

'Never mind him,' she said. 'Tell me more about these fairies.'

'What about your mum, though?' He went pink again. 'What does she think about you coming back? Are they separated, like my folks? My mum moved to Scarborough.'

Saffi knew she could avoid it no longer. 'My mum died last year,' she said. 'Cancer.'

His smile faded. 'I'm so sorry!'

'It's fine. I mean, it's not fine, but it's OK.'

'So it's just you two and your dad.' His gaze was sympathetic. 'Alone.'

'I don't want to talk about it, if you don't mind,' she said.

But even as she spoke, the look on his face changed to one of alarm. She wondered if he saw a spider in her hair. Then, she realised he wasn't watching her at all. He was listening. The wind had stopped.

There was only the crash of waves outside – no whistle.

'I must be going daft,' he muttered.

He rose to his feet, gazing intently at the cave door.

'What is it?' said Saffi, scrambling up as well.

He made no answer. He didn't need to. Something glittered on the sand just outside the cavemouth. It was water, Saffi saw with horror. A bright, snaking line of it crept along the fissure floor, twisting like a living thing.

'Milo!' she called.

She grabbed the yellow bag, hurrying around the outcrop. On the other side, however, she stopped short. The cave had a second exit, a fissure just wide enough for a child. Milo was looking out. She could see a slice of sky above his head. It was cloudless, suffused with pink morning light. How could it be morning? Water welled around Milo's shoes.

'What on earth,' Saffi gasped.

Her brother looked round at her, his face caught by the pink glow. His movements were somehow sluggish. The shape his lips made didn't match the words he was saying. He had a rapt expression.

'It just opened,' he said. 'The door. She's waiting. I see her.'

The pink light was so beautiful that for an instant, Saffi felt an overwhelming urge to rush out to whatever lay beyond. Then, someone pushed roughly past her. Birdy strode over to Milo and grabbed his arm.

'Back the other way!' he told Saffi, curt.

She didn't wait, but stumbled towards the entrance on the far side of the cave. The water lapped around her ankles.

She splashed out into the ordinary grey Yorkshire afternoon, only to find that the sea had covered up the reef. Greedy waves rolled in, gurgling through the gap. Only a narrow strip of pebbles remained at the base of the cliffs.

Birdy pulled a protesting Milo after him. 'Quick. It'll be up to our knees.'

'Let me go!' Milo cried. 'She's waiting. I have to go!'

He appeared to have lost his mind. They both ignored him, edging along by the cliffs, with Birdy keeping a firm grip on Milo's wrist as he kicked and struggled and said some colourful words Saffi didn't realise he knew. Sometimes, they had to walk sideways like crabs, or splash through the shallows. At last, they left the treacherous rocks behind and crunched up the dry shingle of the bay. At the top, Saffi stopped to stare at Birdy. He looked as shaken as she felt.

'It's my fault,' he said. 'Shouldn't have taken you in there.'

'That's OK.' Saffi's heart was hammering hard, as it had by the mirror. 'We lost track of time. Anyone might.'

'It's not just that—' Birdy began.

'You're both dumb.' Milo spat the words. 'Now I can't get back!'

Water had surrounded the point, gleaming and treacherous. Saffi peered into her brother's face. He was flushed, as he had been on the night of their arrival. But this wasn't an ordinary tantrum. He looked almost wild with sadness.

'Who did you see back there?' she asked. 'Who was waiting?' She hadn't seen anyone through the fissure, just the light.

'You know who,' he shouted. 'Her!'

But he wouldn't explain who he meant, or why Saffi would know. Instead, he burst into a bout of furious tears, right there in the middle of the beach.

6
Enemies

This bay was called South Landing, Saffi remembered numbly, trying to comfort Milo. At its head, the beach narrowed to a gulley where fishing boats sat by a concrete slipway. It was busy despite the stiff breeze. Children dug in the sand with spades. A group pushed a red dinghy out in the water. It didn't look like a place to find strange new worlds.

Birdy must have been thinking something similar. He waited until Milo had calmed down and stood glaring at the sea in silence. Then he turned to Saffi.

'That pink light,' he said. 'That weren't anywhere in Holderness. Nor in this world, I reckon.'

Saffi gave a reluctant nod. 'It was magic.'

'*Her* magic.' Milo didn't turn around to speak, his fists balled at his sides. 'And you two went and ruined it.'

'We don't know who you mean, Milo,' Saffi said as gently as she could.

'Yes, you do,' he snapped. 'In the mirror, at home. All dressed in white. You saw her. Don't pretend you didn't.'

'But that wasn't—' began Saffi.

'A lady?' Birdy was gazing at them both intently. 'You saw a lady in white at Fortune House?' He made a gesture at his face. 'Beautiful? Green eyes?'

'You know her?' Saffi said in surprise.

Birdy had gone pale. 'So she's here,' he murmured.

Then he turned abruptly away, walking at a great pace up the beach. Saffi had to hurry after him, panting out her question while Milo trailed in the rear.

'You know about this lady?'

'A legend.' Birdy strode along. 'Folk see her. A woman in white, riding a white horse – the "White Lady". Some say she's the Fairy Queen.' He shot Saffi a glance. 'If you saw her at Fortune House, be careful. That's powerful magic.'

Saffi remembered the woman watching them from the first-floor window, and shuddered. A strong suspicion had begun to form in her mind regarding those guests. But Milo was unconvinced.

'It's not fairies,' he called from behind. 'Fairies are stupid girly things.'

'Not these ones,' Birdy warned.

Saffi ignored the seven-year-old's insights. 'How about we go over what we've seen so far.' She caught hold of Birdy's arm, slowing him down. 'Step by step. When was the first time we saw magic, before the cave? Milo's right. There was a face in the mirror. I don't know whose,' she added as her brother whooped with triumph. 'It was too quick for me.'

'Also the frame,' he said. 'And the wallpaper.'

'And before that, the bell.' Saffi frowned. 'Wait, no. That wasn't the first thing. Last night, I got up because I was curious about the guests. The stairs played a trick on me. It took forever to go down, then I skipped a bunch. It was weird.'

'Don't forget the pictures.' Milo was insistent. 'And the food.'

'If that's fairy food, best not eat it,' said Birdy.

He seemed plunged in gloom, as if this was all bad news. But another idea had occurred to Saffi. She halted on the shingle so the others had to stop and face her.

'Grandma said that!' Her excitement was mounting. 'Don't you see? They *know*. Grandma and Grandad. About the magic. I don't think Dad does. And those guests – they're behind it all, I swear. Everything started after they arrived.'

She appealed to Milo. 'I know you don't like it, but I think they're fairies. That's who Grandad meant. He said *she'll be offended.* She – the White Lady. She wants to meet Dad. I even saw her at an upstairs window.'

Birdy was nodding but Milo scowled. 'You never told me that,' he said.

He picked up a fistful of pebbles and began lobbing them furiously at the water. There was no point in arguing with him. They had reached the widest part of the bay by now, surrounded by rippling shallows and water-streaked sands. Grey clouds massed over the sea; Saffi thought it might rain. One problem bothered her.

'Why now?' she muttered. 'Why didn't they come before?'

'You said it,' Birdy pointed out. 'They're here to talk to your dad.'

The business of the guests was beginning to make a dim sort of sense to Saffi. In any case, it explained why Dad and Grandad were arguing. Milo meanwhile had worked himself up into a froth, chucking rocks at the distance.

'You're both wrong!' he cried. 'It's not fairies. It's – it's—'

Then he broke off again, frustrated. Saffi couldn't tell whether he was unwilling to say what he meant, or unable.

'All right, Milo,' she said patiently. 'If not fairies, what?'

'A message from another world,' he replied at once.

'What kind of message?'

But Milo wouldn't meet her eye. She was sure that there was something else he wasn't telling her. She watched him a second longer before turning back to Birdy.

'Sir Henry's deal doesn't explain the cave,' she said. 'Have you ever seen a light like that, Birdy?'

His expression grew troubled. 'Not exactly . . .'

He trailed off and didn't finish. Saffi was about to ask again, when a familiar sight caught her gaze. She and Birdy were facing the boats pulled up at the head of the beach. A number of birds had landed on the upturned craft to perch on the wooden keel, beady eyes on them. There were seagulls, crows, a magpie, a few terns. It was just like the scene in town – the one she thought she had dreamed. As she watched, two herring gulls flapped down to stalk over the pebbles. A crow did the same.

Saffi positioned herself between the gulls and Milo, wary of those sharp hooked beaks. 'What's going on?' she whispered to Birdy.

His face was hard to read. He said nothing about the birds but pointed towards the gully at the head of the bay, as if they were discussing the way home.

'Past time we started back, if you want to beat rain,' he said.

Then he strolled on up the beach. He obviously had his reasons. Saffi herded Milo after him. To her relief, the birds didn't follow. Her brother was in a terrible mood, dragging along with a scowl as if the story of the White Lady was a personal insult. Saffi decided to let him cool off. The events in the cave had been a shock. She felt light-headed herself.

It was strange to pass people in shorts and flipflops on the slipway, ordinary families headed for the beach on a summer's day. But the world carried on, fairy magic or no fairy magic. Her watch read almost three o'clock. Again, she hadn't seen the time pass. Birdy led them to the foot of an escarpment covered with yellow flowers, where flights of wooden steps led to the clifftop. It was a long climb. At the top, they stopped to catch their breath, gazing out over wheatfields. The path continued westwards, wriggling along the headlands. Birdy stopped then, peering at the sky.

'Listen,' he said, low and soft. 'You're in grave danger. You and Milo. That magic – it doesn't like to be talked about. Birds are a sign.'

'Why just us?' Saffi felt hot from the climb, irritated. 'It's you the gull attacked.'

'Them in town are always mardy. Might not be the same thing.'

Saffi squinted with distaste at the faraway winged shapes, wheeling over the bay. 'We can't let that stop us. We have to find out what my grandparents know.'

'And if they won't say?' Birdy watched her carefully.

'You mean they'd straight out lie?'

He shrugged. 'Some magic you can't talk about.'

'If it's like that,' she answered, a little deflated, 'I'll snoop. Look for clues. Maybe there's something at the house about this deal of Sir Henry's. Some kind of proof.'

'I'll ask around the village too.' Birdy gave her a hard look. 'Whatever you do, don't talk to those guests.'

'What d'you take me for?'

But Birdy was in an odd mood. He wouldn't let the matter go until she and Milo had promised, standing there on the clifftop with Milo rolling his eyes, that they wouldn't approach their otherworldly guests. After that, he was satisfied.

'I know a short cut to yours,' he told them. 'By my place. Come on.'

Saffi was more than willing. Together, they skirted the wheatfields drenched in afternoon sunlight, following the path along the cliffs. The air was balmy despite the incoming rain, sweet with a smell of ripening wheat. Once, she spied a kestrel hovering on an updraft, but there wasn't anything magical about it aside from its beauty. It hung motionless before folding its wings to drop. As to Birdy, he limited himself to remarks about their surroundings. It turned out their houses were barely a mile apart, separated by a few fields. They would pass by his on the way, though he didn't go so far as to invite them in. At a fork in the path, he turned right, following a signpost to Flamborough village.

But when they approached a lot between the fields containing rows of caravans, Saffi noticed a change in him. He became silent and watchful, walking along a lane bordered by a sparse hedge. The Lythe holiday park was a modest affair, a pasture capable of holding about two dozen vehicles, reached via a driveway behind a rundown bungalow. The pitches weren't even a third full, while the shower block had a sign that said *out of order*. Birdy passed the driveway, turning left onto a farmer's track.

'Fortune House is straight on,' he said.

Just as they drew level with the bungalow's back garden, Milo chose to ask a question in his fluting voice.

'Is this the place Grandad wants to buy?'

Birdy grimaced. 'Not so loud,' he whispered.

'Why?' asked Milo.

He hadn't been with them when they discussed it. Birdy didn't answer. He looked stricken, his gaze fixed on the bungalow. A moment later, Saffi saw why. A man had come into view, seated on a plastic chair by a brick-built kiosk. With his greasy hair and stained tracksuit, he gave off an impression of furious sadness. The kiosk with its metal roller blind was the sort of camp shop that sold crisps and toilet paper. Several beer cans sat on the ground by the man. He drank one while checking his phone.

'Chuffin' 'eck,' Birdy muttered.

Saffi understood, with a prickle of discomfort, that this was his father. Birdy moved on with a tread so light that he might have been made of air. Unfortunately, Mr Lythe was facing the hedge and caught sight of them.

'Look who it is.' His voice carried across the garden. 'And not yet teatime.'

Birdy halted. His expression shut down as his father approached, all emotion gone. Saffi was surprised by the transformation.

'Who's this lot then.' Mr Lythe glowered at Saffi and Milo. 'Picking up strays, lad?'

There was no 'hello', or 'ey up'. Even Grandad's moods hadn't prepared Saffi for this person who gazed stony-faced at them over the hedge. Before Birdy could answer, Milo did – in the worst possible way.

'My name's Milo,' he piped. 'We're staying at—'

'A B&B,' Saffi said quickly. 'We're up from London. Pleased to meet you.'

For an instant, Mr Lythe looked as if she had said they were from Mars. Then – it was more frightening than the glower – he burst into a loud, long laugh.

'Up from London, eh,' he guffawed. 'And us the lucky ones.' He turned to Birdy, the laugh gone. 'Enough tourist-guiding, lad. You're needed at shop.'

Birdy didn't argue with his father. He gave Saffi an apologetic look. 'How about we meet up tomorrow? I'll come to yours . . .'

But Mr Lythe wasn't going to make it easy on them. 'You're wanted here tomorrow,' he said. 'I've a delivery in Hull.'

'So.' Birdy kept his gaze on Saffi. 'I'll see you round.'

He was trying to tell her something without spelling it out, giving her a meaningful look. Saffi guessed she could come by while his father was out.

Mr Lythe's black eyebrows bristled. 'Happen you will, happen you won't,' he rumbled. 'Your throne awaits.' He pointed Birdy towards the kiosk, before giving Saffi a mocking salute. 'Sithee, London.'

He hadn't missed that she kept back her name. Birdy had no choice but to squeeze through a gap in the hedge. He threw her a final look as he followed his dad. After that, they disappeared around a corner, and Saffi and Milo were alone. A wind stirred the tree branches. Dark clouds rolled in.

'Well, that's that,' Saffi sighed.

She turned and walked on with Milo, following the farmer's track Birdy had said would lead to Fortune House. Even with a shortcut she doubted they would get there before the rain. It was frustrating to lose their new friend so quickly.

'Why d'you lie to his dad?' Milo asked after a while.

'He can't know who we are,' Saffi said. 'He hates Trues because of this bad property deal with Grandad.'

Milo accepted the explanation readily enough. She supposed it wasn't difficult to imagine someone hating Grandad – though he had met his match in Mr Lythe. It occurred to her that Birdy might have worse problems than fairies.

The storm, when it struck about ten minutes later, did so in spectacular fashion. The rain started just as they arrived on the far side of a pasture, at a lane. All at once, the sky opened up and they were both wet through in seconds. Saffi recognised the road to the B&B. As they trudged on, sloshing through puddles, she heard a car engine behind them, and turned to see Dad's blue Skoda, crawling through the downpour.

'Well, well. What a pair of drowned rats,' he said, rolling down a window.

He had been in town all day, he told them, making enquiries at the Council about the B&B. But he was in a good mood for a change as they climbed in the back, streaming water on the seat.

'Your grandma'll lose her mind,' he chuckled. 'She hates wet clothes.'

'Dad,' Saffi said as they passed by the B&B gates. 'I need to ask you something. We've had a weird day.'

'Fire away.'

But Milo chimed in before she could continue. 'Mum's sending us messages from heaven,' he announced. 'She's changing things at the house.'

To hear it spelled out like that was a shock to Saffi,

though she had guessed he was still obsessed by his ghosts. The shock made her angry.

'That's not true,' she said. Milo scowled at her.

'All right.' Dad sighed as he pulled up by the front door. 'Seems we need a family talk. I've been ignoring you two lately, right? Forgive me. I've a bunch of things on my mind, and none of them are as important as you.'

He switched off the engine and turned to them, smiling. 'This is normal. The counsellor told us. We'll see things, hear things. It's because she's still here.' He tapped his heart. 'Inside.'

'Not that.' Milo blushed. 'I mean real messages. Saffi's seen them, too.'

Saffi shook her head. 'That's not what it was.'

'Says you!' Milo was close to tears again. 'Because you won't believe in it, even when it's right in front of you. You prefer some stupid fairy story. I hate you!'

With that, he threw open the car door and ran through the rain to the house, slamming the door behind him. Saffi and her father were left in dazed silence.

'Don't worry,' Dad said. 'I'll go talk to him.'

'He's right,' said Saffi as they both got out of the car. 'Just not about Mum. Weird stuff's been happening.'

'Such as?'

She walked after him to the door, arm crooked over her head against the rain. 'We saw something in a beach cave. A door to another world. It was real, Dad.'

The familiar leaf smell greeted her as she stepped inside,

mixed with something new: a sharp, musky odour, like an animal. Saffi stood on the doormat, droplets trickling down her cheeks. The pictures of Mum were still missing. Milo must have gone up to their room, as his anorak and trainers lay in a wet heap by the stairs. Dad gave her an odd look as he hung up his mac by the door.

'A door to another world,' he repeated.

'Sounds silly. But that's what it was. Milo says he saw someone in there. And that's not all.' She kicked off her sodden trainers. 'What's going on here? Who are these guests? Have you met them?'

She had been prepared for disbelief. What she didn't expect was the flash of anger in his eyes.

'Did your grandfather put you up to this?' he said.

Saffi was too surprised to say anything. Just then, a door closed in the kitchen and Grandma's voice rose up.

'. . . Baths,' she was protesting. 'We'll be heating up coppers, traipsing up and down stairs like it's eighteen-hundred!'

'If you want someone to blame, I suggest that son of yours.' Grandad's reply was surly. 'Longer he waits, worse it gets. He's the heir.'

Saffi tore her eyes away from Dad to see Grandma arriving, her apron covered in flour as if she had been baking again. She halted when she saw them. Behind her, Grandad appeared, holding a pair of pliers.

'Boiler's broken,' Grandma said, apologetic. 'We'll have to heat—'

Dad cut her off. 'Mother, Father. May I have a word?'

He had moved behind Saffi, putting his hands on her shoulders in a protective way. It was probably meant well, but made her feel trapped.

'Out all day. *Now* his lordship wants a word,' said Grandad.

'I'd like to know what you've been saying to my daughter.' Dad's voice was calm but Saffi could hear the edge in it. 'What you've told her about Fortune House.'

'I don't know what you mean.' Grandad's expression had grown as thunderous as the storm.

'We agreed to leave the children out of this. That was my one condition.'

'I've said nowt to the lass.'

'William. Why don't you let Saffi change?' Grandma hovered between them, anxious. 'She'll catch her death in those wet clothes. Where's Milo?'

The others ignored her. Saffi wanted desperately to leave, but was stuck listening to yet another sparring match between her father and grandfather. Then, she stiffened. Ever so fleeting – she would have missed it, if she hadn't been looking straight at it – a hairy muzzle poked out from under the grandfather clock. Were there rats in the B&B, on top of everything else?

'I don't believe you,' Dad was saying. 'Filling her head with this nonsense – magic doors and whatnot – after all that palaver with Anoush. Years she spent on this stupid story of yours. And now you start again.'

'Your wife,' Grandad snapped back, 'was a damn sight

more sensible than you are. If you'd listened to her, we wouldn't be having this conversation today.'

'Stop it!' said Saffi suddenly.

She wrenched free of Dad and turned to face them both.

'Just stop,' she told them. 'No one's said anything, Dad. I saw things. So did Milo. I don't suppose you noticed while you were busy being mad at each other, but he's having a hard time. You're not helping.'

Without waiting for an answer, she marched upstairs. Arriving in the bedroom, she found Milo bundled underneath his quilt, jeans dumped on the floor. She sat down beside him on the bed.

'Sorry about earlier.' She sighed. 'I was surprised and it came out wrong. What makes you so sure it's Mum?'

'Because.' His voice was muffled by the bedclothes. 'I saw her.'

'In the mirror? I thought so too, but—'

'No.' His blotched and tear-stained face peeped out from under the quilt. 'Through that door in the cave. She was waiting for us. See why I wanted to go, Saf?'

7
A Visit

No matter how much Saffi argued the point with him after that, Milo clung to his theory about Mum. When she told him it didn't seem right to find heaven in a cave, he turned his face to the wall and said no more about it, or indeed anything else for the rest of the afternoon. When he finally got dressed and came down for tea, he was as quiet as he had been during the worst days with Mum. Saffi was at a loss as to how to comfort him. Dad was no help. After the argument in the hall, he disappeared into the study and emerged only when it was time to eat.

By then, his quarrel with Grandad had entered the cold war stage. The evening meal – soggy fish and chips – passed in silence, broken by Grandma's chatter and the bell. This rang several times for hot water, which had to be boiled and carried upstairs. Saffi wondered what use magical creatures could have for so many baths. Despite being run off her feet, Grandma was the only member of the family who managed to be cheerful. Once or twice, Saffi worked herself up to the point of asking her about the Lady. But every time, the bell rang, or the kettle boiled, or something needed to be taken out of the oven.

After the meal, Dad called Saffi into the study to apologise for the atmosphere at home, because, as he put it: 'grown-ups sometimes behave like small children.' But he wouldn't explain what he said about Mum.

'That's an old story.' He waved her away. 'I'll tell you one day. When I'm less busy.'

Saffi knew when she was being fobbed off. Dad wasn't busy. He wasn't teaching – wasn't even writing a book as far as she could tell, despite spending all that time in the study. The papers about the *White Hind*, she noted, had been tidied away.

The next day, a Thursday, was no better. Though Dad and Grandad didn't argue again, the row poisoned everything. Grandad went about with a martyred air. Dad wolfed down breakfast and disappeared in the study. As to Grandma, she must have felt that the best way to deal with family problems was to ignore them completely and plunge into housework. All morning, she was baking, boiling, running up and down stairs. The silver bell seemed to ring on a continual basis. Their mysterious visitors never left their rooms, though Saffi sometimes heard echoes of voices or laughter. As her grandparents wouldn't allow her to take anything up to the guest suite, there wasn't much she could do to help.

She vowed not to let it keep her from her search. Finally, by dint of waiting and watching for the right moment, she cornered Grandad alone in the basement. He was kneeling by the broken boiler, shining a torch behind the cylinder.

'Grandad,' she began. 'What's going on? Who are those guests?'

'You heard your father,' he said, sour. 'I'm to keep mouth shut about this house and all in it. If you want truth, ask him. About time he faced it.'

'He says he's too busy.'

This reply drew a snort of disbelief from her grandfather. But he said nothing, wrestling the pipes behind the boiler with a wrench.

'Please,' she tried again. 'At least tell me what he meant about Mum.'

When her grandfather withdrew from behind the boiler, she saw in surprise that he looked sad.

'I'll say this much,' he replied. 'Your mum was a clever woman, though we had our differences. For that, your father blames me.'

'You mean, differences about the guests?'

He gave her a level stare from under bushy eyebrows. 'Leave well alone, lass.'

That was all she could extract from him. But the titbit about differences fired her imagination. Had Mum known about the magic? What did she and Grandad disagree about? It was frustrating not to know. Though she recalled her promise to Birdy, she found herself eyeing the door to the upstairs suite. She wished her family would trust her with the truth – or failing that, let her see it for herself.

At the same time, she began to have an inkling of the danger. That same morning, after Grandma had taken up her umpteenth copper kettle, Saffi happened to pass the landing and find the green door open. She couldn't resist peeping in. Beyond it was a hallway also carpeted in green, where someone had left a fur coat draped on a chair. It was golden, like a lion's pelt; she rather hoped it wasn't real. She heard the sound of low laughter and a splash, as if somebody was in a bath. Even as the thought crossed her mind, she realised she had taken a few steps down the corridor.

They were steps she never meant to take. She backed hastily out, remembering the stair magic. She wouldn't be caught that way again.

She had planned a visit to Birdy. But of course it rained, a steady downpour that set in at about ten and didn't stop. Saffi watched the water sluicing down the windows with suspicion. If the weather had turned out to be magic as well, it wouldn't have surprised her. On its bracket in the kitchen, the guest bell rang until she wanted to tear it off the ceiling. Her grandparents were preoccupied by a fresh spate of electrical emergencies. The kettle, iron and lights on the ground floor all failed in quick succession. Even her father was roped in to buy new bulbs, driving to the hardware store in the relentless rain.

When he wasn't running errands for Grandad and Grandma, Dad shut himself away in the study. He even locked the door, as if there was something he didn't want them to see. Once, when Saffi went in to talk to him, she caught him looking at a website with pictures of houses. He clicked away before she could see more.

The rest of the day was equally unsatisfying. She tried looking for clues about Sir Henry, searching all the bookshelves and cabinets. But she didn't know what she was looking for, so it was pointless. On one occasion, walking back through the musky-smelling hall, she thought she saw the furry face again under a chair. It had bright black eyes and looked like a weasel. But when she bent down to check, there was only an old wooden doorstopper.

Milo remained obstinate about Mum. According to his thinking, anything strange at the house was a sign from her.

'We should have gone in,' he insisted. 'At the cave. Now she's sad.'

Saffi gave up arguing with him, eager to talk the matter over with Birdy the following day. But before that, something else happened which would return to haunt her. She fell asleep that night as usual but woke up in the wee hours, in darkness, to hear a faint sound. This time, it wasn't voices.

It was music.

Someone was playing a fiddle in the guest suite. Saffi lay and listened. The music was achingly beautiful, sweet and melancholy. It told a story that lifted up and spiralled down, rose in hope then lost hope before rising again. The melody reminded her of Birdy's flute. She was tempted to get up and open the bedroom door. Her eyes must have adjusted to the darkness, then, for she saw she wasn't the only one with the idea. Milo had left his bed to tiptoe to the door. He stood there with his hand on the knob.

'Milo,' she whispered. 'Go to sleep.'

He was probably half-asleep anyway, because he didn't try to argue but turned and went back to bed. The fiddle ended its plaintive song. Saffi waited until Milo's breathing was soft and regular before allowing herself to drift off once more.

By Friday morning, she had lost all patience with her brother. He was in a foul temper, sniping at her for no reason as he picked at his cereal in the kitchen. When she wouldn't promise to take him back to the cave, he became silently, savagely angry. The breakfast rush was in full swing; the bell danced on its bracket. Grandma and Grandad strode in and out with trays. Just as Grandma took the last one, another bell rang, this time the front door buzzer.

'Mind getting that, love?' she called to Saffi over her shoulder.

Saffi obliged her by going to answer it, though she knew her dad was right there, in the study. The musky scent was less noticeable today but she couldn't shake a sense of being watched. There were no more furniture or wallpaper changes. When she opened up the front door, she realised the rain had stopped. Sun splashed the woods with gold. At least she would be able to visit Birdy.

On the driveway stood a decidedly earthly apparition: Lily Jackson, dressed in a pink floral jacket. At her heels was a toy poodle with a green collar and a manic, panting air. Its eyes looked in two different directions.

'You,' Saffi blurted out.

She had forgotten all about their neighbour. The poodle gave a shrill little yap.

'Good morning.' Lily smirked, as if to say that she was onto Saffi's game, whatever it was. 'I came to see your dad. Is he here?'

Before Saffi could answer, the study door opened. 'How may I help?' asked Dad.

The poodle grew agitated when it saw him, yapping and straining on its lead. 'Hush, Treasure darling,' said Lily, sweeping him into the crook of one arm.

She pushed past Saffi to hold her other hand out to Dad. 'You didn't get my message, I imagine,' she said. 'I'm Lily Jackson. Breakwell High, class of . . . oh, too long ago.' She tittered. 'I live just up the road. I did bring a housewarming gift –' here her gaze strayed to Saffi – 'but it doesn't appear to have been delivered.'

'Is that right, Saf?' Dad turned to her in surprise.

'I put it on the kitchen table—' Saffi began.

But Lily was talking over her. 'A bottle of champers. To celebrate your return. Though you're probably thinking, I've no idea who this Lily person is.'

'No – yes – of course I remember,' said Dad. 'Come in, we'll catch up.'

He ushered Lily in, still carrying Treasure like a lolling handbag. But the look he gave Saffi was full of disappointment. It was mortifying. As the study door clicked shut behind them, the grandfather clock gave a whirring sound, a kind of hiccup, and struck ten. This time, Saffi saw dully, it was running five minutes late.

'True child,' said a husky voice. 'Be strong.'

A shiver went through Saffi. She scanned every corner of the hall. There was no one, no one at all. But she hadn't imagined that voice.

Then she noticed the dining room door. Her grandmother usually kept it shut, in an attempt to dissuade them from going in. Now, it was ajar. Milo's quiet burble rose from the other side. When she peered in, she saw that the doors to one of the display cabinets, the one on the right, were wide open. Milo knelt on the rug under the table. He had taken out some of the figurines and set them up on the rug in a game.

'It's useless,' he whispered. 'She won't see.'

Saffi was about to be a 'big sister' and tell him to put the ornaments away. But she didn't. Why should she care? Milo had chosen to play with statues she disliked, the ones with animal heads. There was a sly cat, a dog baring its teeth, a snarling rat. What she had taken for a doorstopper was one of these ugly things. She could have sworn there were fewer items on the shelves, even counting those Milo took out. Her brother looked up and flushed when he saw her.

'Having fun?' she asked.

He made no reply, because Grandma had arrived downstairs. Saffi heard her long before she came in, commenting on her thought process every step of the way.

'I told you not to go in dining room, my loves – goodness

me, Milo, you've opened cabinet doors – I said – oh dear, not those!'

She bustled past Saffi to snatch up the figurines, putting them hurriedly back. 'These are antiques,' she said. 'Your grandad won't be pleased.'

'I'm not hurting them,' objected Milo.

'All the same. They aren't toys. They're a family legacy.'

Milo scrambled to his feet and ran out of the room.

'What's et him?' Grandma stared, her blue eyes round with concern. 'I hope he's not coming down with 'flu.'

Saffi guessed her grandmother must know something about the fairy magic. Now was her chance to put it to the test.

'Grandma,' she said. 'I know those guests aren't foreigners. Who are they?'

'D'you think he's upset with me?' Her grandmother was still staring after Milo in a flustered way.

Saffi was taken aback. Had Grandma not heard the question? Or had she just chosen to ignore it? She tried again.

'Grandma. Those guests. Where are they from?'

'Don't care for 'em myself,' Grandma chattered on, turning back to the figurines in the cabinet. 'Honestly, have you ever seen such grotesques? But your grandfather would be heartbroken if they broke.'

Only then, gazing at her grandmother's kind, anxious, flour-flecked face, did Saffi understand. It wasn't so much that she didn't have time to pay attention. It was that she couldn't, or wouldn't speak about the guests. Like Birdy said, the magic didn't want to be talked about. Grandma refused to meet her eye as she locked the cabinet with a key from her pocket. Her expression almost begged it. *Don't ask, so I don't have to tell.* It was the first time Saffi had grasped how frightened she was.

'Where's your father got to?' She filled the air with breathless talk, hurrying out of the room ahead of Saffi. 'Grandad wants him.'

But Dad had given them the slip. When they checked the study, it was empty. A note waited for them. *Going for lunch with Lily. Don't wait.*

'He might have told me to my face,' Grandma sighed.

He might have said goodbye, thought Saffi. She had taken a violent dislike to Lily, who was set on worming her way into Dad's good graces. Not that Saffi could do anything about that. Their neighbour was like the bell, or the bulbs, or the boiler, what Grandad called *a test of character*. Something you put up with.

When she went in search of Milo, Saffi found him sprawled on the bedroom rug, brooding over a colouring book.

'I'm going to Birdy's after lunch,' she said. 'Maybe he's got answers. Want to come?'

He shrugged. 'I know the answers.'

Brothers were also a test, Saffi decided. It was useless to try to talk to anyone in her family. They had all backed into their respective corners. But a breakthrough did come at lunch when she least expected it. Dad hadn't yet returned. Grandad also gave their meal of dry ham sandwiches a miss, still battling with the boiler. Muffled curses could be heard drifting through the basement door as Saffi and Milo ate. Or rather, as Saffi ate. Milo didn't touch his food. Grandma was busy mixing up more dough, shaking her head over Grandad.

'I told him,' she said. 'It's old wiring. We need one of those new combi-thingies.'

'Remember Mum's tarts?' Saffi couldn't help saying it, gazing at Grandma's pale dollops of dough. 'She used pears.'

It wasn't the best topic. Milo pulled a long face. Saffi thought Grandma would change the subject. Instead, she beamed with pleasure.

'Queen of fruits. Your mother knew a thing or two.'

That was when Saffi realised she hadn't talked to Grandma about the business with Mum. Even if she refused to mention the guests, she might know why Dad was so upset.

'Why did Dad say those things to Grandad, the other day?' she asked. 'About Mum?'

To her surprise, an answer was forthcoming. 'Oh, I expect he meant the house, the history, all that. Sir Henry. Your mum used to talk about him to your grandfather.'

Saffi couldn't believe what she was hearing. Her gaze met Milo's. He was listening with close attention.

'She never told us,' she said.

'That's because she didn't approve.' Grandma bent down to light the fire box in the stove. 'Grandad makes a great deal out of family pride and whatnot. Your mum took a dim view of same. In my opinion, the truth lies somewhere in between.'

'What didn't she approve of?' asked Saffi.

The answer came from inside the enamel stove, slightly hollow. 'Well. Sir Henry's business dealings, for one. He made a fortune trading for the East India Company. Your mum would write reams to your grandad about it. Until your dad put a stop to that. Said she was tiring herself out.'

'Grandma,' said Saffi carefully. 'Did you keep her letters?'

Grandma straightened up, her face full of sympathy. 'Sorry, lass. We kept them a long time, but William cleared out those boxes last year. If you don't have them, he must have thrown them all away.'

✤ 8 ✤
A Story

Thrown them away, Saffi thought to herself for possibly the tenth time as she left the house. So Mum had been interested in the True family history. She had even written to Grandad about it. And Dad had thrown the letters away. How could he? She would have wanted to keep any last scrap of Mum. Everything her father had done lately struck her as strange, from his pronouncements to Grandad, to going out to lunch with Lily. She didn't understand him.

It was about two o'clock when she set off for Birdy's, without Milo this time. She took the track across the fields, her mac on in case it rained. But for now, the sky was a glorious blue, the beech and oak woods glistening in the sunlight. Everything glittered as if brand new. She was still thinking about Dad's bizarre choices as she reached the Lythe bungalow. Turning up the weed-filled driveway, she glimpsed a familiar blond head in the kiosk.

Birdy was sitting on a stool, slumped over the counter with a bored expression. But when he saw her coming, he scrambled out to meet her.

'I tried to tell you last time,' he said. 'I'd go to yours.'

He seemed anxious, glancing about him as if he expected his father or some other unwanted person to turn up. He pulled her round to the side of the kiosk, out of sight. The plastic chair was in the same spot along with the empty beer cans.

'Oh.' Saffi winced. 'I thought you meant come here.'

'Never mind.' He checked his watch. 'Dad'll be gone a few hours.'

'Does he always make you work like this?' she asked as he fetched a second chair from the kiosk. 'During holidays?'

'It's not that.' He blushed again. His dad was evidently a sore spot. 'He's working three jobs to try and keep park. I have to help out.'

Saffi began to understand, then. It wasn't so much that Birdy's dad was a bully, just that he was desperate. She wished Grandad could see the effect of his 'business' on Birdy. But her discomfort began to ebb as they sat down to compare notes on the fairy deal. They picked up exactly where they had left off, with Sir Henry.

'Wait till you hear what I found,' Birdy said. 'I had to mind shop yesterday, right. But old Ben Wishaw came by – he's a neighbour – and I know he knows the old tales. So I ask him about Sir Henry. Flippin' 'eck! Man was a piece of work. You don't mind me saying that about someone in your family?'

'Only half my family,' Saffi qualified. 'I think my mum guessed stuff about him, too, because she didn't like him. Go on.'

'It starts off how we know.' He lowered his voice. 'Young Henry's just an ordinary mug, son of a cottager. Dreams of making his fortune at sea. One night, All Hallows' Eve, he takes a shortcut home. Who should he see at crossroads but a troop of the Fair Folk, all kitted out with bells on their saddles and bells on their reins. At their head, a Lady on a white horse – most beautiful thing you've ever seen. Henry's surprised, as you'd imagine. But he's no fool. He's heard tales of the White Lady, how she'll grant wishes. So he hides. When she's close, he reaches out to grab her by the silver stirrup.

'"Why do you hold me back, son of man?" she says.

'"I'll let go when you grant me wishes three," he answers with the old phrase.

'She warns him that what he asks comes at a price. He says he'll pay. First, he wishes for a ship. This she gives. Then, he wishes to make a fortune. This she gives as well. Last, he wishes for Fortune House, to pass that luck on to his heirs. This she also grants though she says he won't live to enjoy it. It all happens as she says. He makes his fortune in trade. Gets a bit of a reputation. No one bests Sir Henry in business, certainly not the people he cheats and swindles. He comes back knighted. Marries a local lady.'

'And?' Saffi felt a little breathless.

'This is the bit I didn't know.' Birdy dropped his voice to a whisper. 'You'd think he'd be happy, right? But his wife disappears. Family says she died, but there's rumours of worse. He gets odd, talks about curses and magic. Finally, he tries to burn down Fortune House. It half works. Upstairs burns but downstairs stays. After that, he goes proper barmy. Keeps taking off clothes to jump in sea. And get this.' He gave Saffi a significant look. 'He thinks he's the one on fire. Ends his days in loony bin. Like that house took revenge.'

A knot of worry had begun to twist in Saffi's stomach as Birdy told his tale. Somehow, she expected Sir Henry's good fortune to last longer.

'Any chance this is Old Ben's especially spooky version?' she asked.

'Maybe,' Birdy said. 'But it's not over. So. Fortune House half burns down. But the son still owns the place. Finally, he rebuilds it. Starts acting like his father did: cruel, greedy, grasping. Says he wants to bring glory to the True name. After that, it's always the same. Every generation, Trues make their fortune. And they always keep Fortune House.'

'Wait.' Saffi half rose, struck by an idea. 'Grandad said that. *Every generation . . .*'

At that precise moment – she hadn't been paying attention to anything else, absorbed in Birdy's story – it happened. A dark shape whizzed by her head. Birdy ducked just in time to avoid the jackdaw that divebombed the kiosk. It flew straight into the brick wall and landed at their feet, legs splayed out, stunned. Then it shook itself and took off again.

Birdy jumped up. 'Into the house!' he cried.

Even as he said it, Saffi saw shapes wheeling in a sky that had been empty seconds before. Big and little, dark and light. The birds! She pelted after Birdy, making for the back door.

Something skimmed past her ear – a huge magpie, bigger than a cat. It flapped directly over Birdy's head, claws outstretched, screeching. It continued to harry him until they reached the door and burst into the bungalow's dim kitchen. Birdy slammed the door. Once, twice, a flapping, scrabbling shape banged against the frosted glass. Then, all was quiet. Saffi realised she was holding her breath and let go.

'That'll teach us,' panted Birdy. 'From now on, magic talk is inside. OK?'

He had a long red scratch down one cheek. It didn't escape Saffi that every time their feathered nemeses attacked, they were bent on hurting him.

The Lythe kitchen, she noticed, was a dowdy place, with empty tins and beer bottles piled on the counters. Birdy must have seen it, too, for he glanced about him in embarrassment before leading her to his bedroom. This was no bigger than the one Saffi used to have in London, with most of the space taken up by a bed and chest of drawers. The superhero duvet and lampshade were meant for a younger boy, while the metal bed squeaked when they sat down. But there was no sign of birds when they looked out of the window. The sky was clear, the garden deserted.

'You're bleeding,' she told Birdy.

He touched his cheek, looking surprised when his fingers came away red. 'No worse than brambles.'

'Why do they always go for you?' she asked as they scanned the garden, kneeling on the bed together.

'Guess I'm the lucky one.' He sounded like his father. 'One thing's for sure. They don't like us talking about Trues.'

Saffi nodded. 'And I know why the Lady wants to see Dad.'

Briefly, she explained her realisation before the birds attacked – that Sir Henry's deal was passed down the generations. Every True heir had either to accept or reject it. But her father didn't believe in magic. He didn't even want to meet the guests. She couldn't help thinking that was a risky position to take. Birdy agreed.

'You've got to warn him,' he said. 'He can't just ignore it, he'll offend them. They're finicky that way. Maybe he'll listen to you.'

They talked for a while after that, discussing the True deal in whispers, crouched side by side on the superheroes. According to Old Ben's telling, a fairy contract was a tricky thing, full of rules and conditions. Breaking any of these invited reprisals. Saffi was certain Grandma lived in fear of it. But when she told Birdy about Mum's letters and her disappointment with Dad, his response was thoughtful.

'He was sad. I felt the same after my mum went. Not,' he added in haste, 'as I hold it against her.'

'It's annoying though. I feel like I'm missing part of her.'

He gave her one of his keen looks. 'And a part of her is a part of you.'

Saffi hadn't put it like that, but he was right. Missing out on Mum's letters was like losing a piece of herself. The lump rose in her throat.

'I'm sorry,' he said.

But his gaze had strayed to the window and kiosk outside. He was obviously thinking about his own father. It was time, in any case, for her to go home and speak with hers. Dad had to see reason. She and Birdy agreed to meet again tomorrow, in town, where he had permission to busk by the bingo hall.

'What if something happens before that?' she asked.

His answer was ready. 'We go to the other one's house.'

That was how they left it. Though she squinted a long time at the sky before stepping outside, Saffi set off for the B&B with a lighter heart after their talk. She had begun to feel Birdy was the only one she could turn to. Milo was a dead loss. She had been too embarrassed to mention his cave theory; it felt uncomfortable, as if by calling Mum a ghost, they were being disloyal. There were other things to worry about. Returning home by the field paths, she kept glancing upwards in a nervous reflex. Black dots circled high overhead. At times, a seagull cut through the rest like a pale knife. She was aware of those winged watchers, wheeling and sweeping through the skies all the way back.

If she was expecting trouble at Fortune House, however, she didn't find it. Everything was much the same as when she left. Grandma, deep in her mixing bowls in the kitchen, informed her that Grandad and Dad had gone out hardware-buying.

'Fuses,' she said darkly, as if these were malevolent beings.

'Where's Milo?' Saffi asked.

'Upstairs, love. Colouring.'

Saffi hurried off to talk to her brother. She passed by the green door on her way to the bedrooms, starting up the flight to the second floor. Then, she did a double take. She was still by the green door. The stairs had played their trick on her again.

Suddenly, she felt irritated rather than afraid. She wanted to tell Milo about Sir Henry – she wanted to confront Dad. She had no time for stupid fairy stairs.

'Stop it,' she said, stamping her foot.

There was no answer. The stairs stretched on ahead, peaceful and ordinary. She took one cautious step, then another. Everything was normal.

Maybe she had shown the magic she wasn't afraid. Or else it was mocking her.

When she reached the bedroom, she found Milo where she had left him, on the rug with his crayons. He didn't look up from a picture of a triceratops, which he had coloured deep green.

'It's fairies,' she announced flatly. 'Sir Henry made a deal with the White Lady. Trues renew it every generation.'

After hearing the story, Milo wasn't as opposed as she had expected. But he did have one addition and stuck to it.

'I don't see why it can't be both,' he said. 'Fairies and Mum. She's sending us messages. Fairies bring them, like the post.'

'Whatever it is, it's dangerous.'

'You're worried about nothing,' said Milo.

Saffi wasn't convinced. That evening she was impatient for her dad to come home. She felt that time was running out, that she must speak to him before it was too late. But it was six o'clock before her father and grandfather returned. By then, Saffi was in the kitchen, helping Grandma make tea. Dad and Grandad must have argued again for Dad looked gloomy as he stepped in the back door, giving Saffi a perfunctory hug.

'Later,' he said when she asked to talk. 'I have to finish up a few things.'

He disappeared into the study again. Grandad had stalked off to the basement in silence. Neither of them came back when Grandma served up the food. Milo also greeted the rubbery egg and chips on his plate with dismay.

'They look like plastic,' he said.

'Ah?' Grandma shoved another tray of tarts in the oven, her patience frayed. 'So, cook your own.'

As she spoke, the guest bell, which had been unusually silent, gave its peremptory jingle-jangle. Grandma cast a weary glance up at it.

'Lord help me. If I'm not back in ten, Saf, could you take this batch out?'

Milo pushed his plate away when Grandma left.

'I'm not hungry.'

'You could be nicer to her,' said Saffi. 'She's got a lot on her mind.'

He gave her a strange look. If she had to describe it, she would have said he resembled an old-fashioned princeling, proud and cold. It was a closed-faced, small-eyed, uncaring look.

'It's her one job,' he snapped. 'To care for us. She can't even do that.'

He got up and strode out, leaving Saffi at a loss as to what had brought all this on. After a few minutes, when Grandma didn't return, she rescued the tarts from the oven and set them on the counter. Then she went to fetch the pastry box.

But when she opened up the pantry door, she had to bite her lip so as not to scream. There on the shelf, seated beside the dish of salmon and swinging its legs as it nibbled on a jam tart, was the strangest creature she had ever seen. She guessed it must be a fairy: a being about the size of a stoat with red hair pulled up in a bun, furred hands and feet, large black eyes and a long, snuffling nose. It wore an old-fashioned dress with ruffles in a blue forget-me-not pattern. As Saffi watched in amazement, it stood up, clasped its claws together and dropped her a polite curtsy.

'Well met, True child,' it said in a husky voice she remembered. 'My name is Piccola. I come bearing a message. My Lady sends greetings. She also requests the pleasure of your company. You are to visit her tomorrow morning, at nine, in her apartments.'

9

An Invitation

Having delivered the message, the creature stood waiting. Saffi realised through her haze of shock that she was supposed to answer. She had never thought fairies could be furred and clawed, yet at the same time so prim. The way the weasel-woman stood there, courteous and attentive, made her want to laugh.

She wasn't fool enough to do so. *Finicky,* she remembered.

'I'm honoured,' she brought out. 'But what does the Lady want with me?'

Piccola's eyes widened. 'Are you not the True heir?'

'I guess,' Saffi said. 'But isn't my dad the heir, ah, first?'

Piccola gave a brief nod. 'Alas, he has forgotten himself. He displeases the Lady. Nine o'clock sharp, room 2A. Do not be late, child.'

Then she was gone, whisking away in the blink of an eye. Saffi couldn't follow the blur of movement. She left the pantry, feeling dazed. So Dad had offended their guests. That couldn't be good. Grandma was back in the kitchen by now, fretting as usual over the stove. Saffi didn't trouble her with the news of the invitation. It was time for her father to step up. She went straight to the study.

She found Dad intent on something he had laid out on the desk. He looked up quickly when she came in but was relieved to see her. He was reading a glossy sales brochure, she noticed, the kind that showed houses with manicured gardens under vivid blue skies. No English sky was ever that blue.

'Dad,' she began.

He spoke at the same time. 'Hello, love. How was your day?'

'Great.' Now, she had to ask him. 'And yours?'

'Informative.' He was pleased about something.

'I wanted to say.' Saffi paused, distracted. 'Why d'you have those?'

She reached for a brochure. *Exceptional lifestyles. Luxury real estate.* Dad didn't have money to buy a place like this.

'Nothing.' He looked guilty. 'A bit of research is all.'

'Dad. I'm not stupid.'

'Fine.' He sighed. 'Just don't tell your grandad. Lily and I have been talking. I've had an idea. It might just be the making of us.'

He took the brochure from her with a conspiratorial air. On the back, Saffi saw with distaste, was a photo of the blonde and smiling Ms Jackson. Under that was the line, *Buy and sell in Breakwell.* Their neighbour was an estate agent.

Then, the awful realisation struck.

'No.' She stared at her father in horror. 'You're not thinking of selling. Not Fortune House. Dad!'

'We were just bouncing figures around,' he said, defensive. 'She's so helpful. Gave me a ballpark price, marketing costs, commission . . .'

Saffi felt her mouth go dry. 'Grandad won't let you. Ever.'

'She explained everything,' he barrelled on. 'A property like this would fetch a cool million. It could set us all up. Your grandparents in their place, us in ours . . .'

'You can't sell Fortune House,' whispered Saffi.

But the look in his eye was glazed. He didn't understand her, and she was beginning to suspect why. This was powerful magic. To sell Fortune House was the ultimate insult to the Lady. She must be punishing him.

'I'll have to work on your grandad a bit.' He went on as if he hadn't heard. 'But Grandma might listen. They're not getting any younger . . .'

'Dad,' Saffi begged. 'Will you do something for me? A small thing.'

He must have seen how desperate she was, because he stopped. 'What?'

'Would you at least try talking to the guests?'

He stared blankly at her. 'What guests, darling?'

The book-lined walls of the study shifted around Saffi, along with the pit of her stomach. *No, no,* she thought.

'The ones upstairs,' she cried, unable to believe her ears.

'There aren't any guests. You'd see their coats.'

'Are you saying you don't hear this?'

Saffi strode to the study door, throwing it wide so that the sound of the jangling bell was loud and clear. Moments later, Grandma hurried upstairs.

'Ah,' Dad said vaguely. 'I suppose they just arrived. What does it matter?'

Then, Saffi remembered what Piccola told her. Dad had *forgotten himself.* The forgetting appeared to be literal. She argued the point several times with him after that, to no avail. He would hear the bell, realise there was someone upstairs, then promptly forget again. After a while, close to tears of fury and frustration, Saffi ran down to the basement to find her grandfather.

'Dad doesn't remember the guests,' she blurted out when she saw him.

Grandad was kneeling by the boiler, tightening a joint. But he gave her a keen glance.

'I was afraid of that,' he answered. 'Don't fret, lass. It's temporary—'

At that point, the joint he had tightened burst, sending a plume of water into the air. Saffi backed away.

'Later,' he called over a squall of water. 'I'll explain.'

Saffi was glad to know Dad's state was temporary. But as evening wore on, she realised she would have to wait for the rest of Grandad's explanations. The magic of the house was definitely mocking them. No sooner had he fixed one thing – boiler, pipes – then another broke. That night, the electricity failed again. They had candles to light them to bed. As to Milo, all he could offer, once Saffi told him about the invitation, was complaints.

'Why you and not me?' he said. 'I want to meet those guests.'

'We can't cause offence. Look what happened to Dad.'

They were already in bed, though Saffi wasn't sleepy. She tossed this way and that, restless. Across the room, Milo exhaled in frustration.

'That's just Mum. She's angry with him.'

'Come on.' Saffi groaned. 'Mum wouldn't do anything to hurt us.'

'That Lady knows,' he said, sullen. 'I bet she's friends with Mum.'

After that he wouldn't talk, sulking with his face turned away. He must have fallen asleep, though, for soon his breathing was deep and regular. Saffi heard him mumble something about strawberries. She lay awake a long while before she could do the same. Grandad would never allow a sale, she was sure of that. But there was no telling what Dad would try in his state. Now, all that time spent with Lily made sense.

Only one option remained, as far as she could see. She would have to plead his case tomorrow with the Lady.

The next day was overcast; Saffi awoke to find dim light seeping through the curtains. She felt very much as if she hadn't slept at all. The first thing she remembered was Dad. The second was her appointment.

'The Lady,' she gasped, throwing off her covers.

She fumbled for her watch on the table, to find with relief that it wasn't yet eight. Milo didn't stir when she shook him. It was just as well. This way, he wouldn't fuss. She dressed and left the room quietly.

Downstairs, she couldn't help it: she had to stop again. The magic changes were flagrant in the hall. The wallpaper had shifted to grey-blue, the tiles to purple. Instead of a musky odour, the place smelled of salty air. There were even puddles of seawater by the stairs. Saffi saw a purple strand in one – seaweed, she realised in bemusement. The study door was open but Dad was nowhere in sight. Grandma was, as ever, in the kitchen, at her most flustered and voluble. Both men, she complained to Saffi, had abandoned her. Grandad was out buying more parts for the boiler. Dad had left to make enquiries at the estate agent's.

'Gone soft in the head, he has, with this house business,' she fumed. 'Your grandad's not going to like it. Not one little bit.'

Saffi could only sit nibbling on a piece of toast, and hope that Dad's actions wouldn't make their situation worse. The next hour was simultaneously the longest and shortest of her life. She watched the hands on the kitchen clock crawl towards nine, wondering what she was going to say to the Lady. Grandma avoided any mention of their visitors. Twice, the bell danced on its bracket. Twice, she hurried off without the least remark.

Finally, at five to nine, Saffi set out for the hall. But she hadn't counted on how conflicted Grandma could be about the guests. She was coming down as Saffi went up, and paused on the stairs.

'Off to wake Milo?' she asked. Her cheeks were red with effort.

Saffi tried the truth one more time. 'The Lady wants to see me, Grandma.'

Fear and love battled visibly in Grandma's face. Finally, she gave in. 'I don't want you going up there,' she whispered. 'Stay away, you hear?'

'I can't refuse.' Saffi was relieved to have a proper exchange on the subject at last. 'They asked for me. An invitation.'

'You can delay it,' Grandma pleaded. 'Your father did.'

'I don't think that worked out for him, do you?'

Grandma looked anguished. 'He went about it wrong. There's rules, a protocol. At least wait for your grandad—'

She had taken a step towards Saffi, reached out a trembling hand. But she must have put a foot wrong for she lurched sideways, grabbing at the banister. It was no use. As Saffi watched in horror, her grandmother tumbled down the flight and landed with a sickening thud at the bottom. In the silence that followed, Saffi could have sworn she heard a mean chuckle in the hall. *Fairies*, she thought grimly, hastening down.

'Are you all right?' she asked, kneeling on the floor.

Grandma was in pain, that much was clear. But she showed with gestures that she wanted Saffi to help her sit up, so she couldn't have broken too many bones. Her right ankle was swelling visibly under its brown stocking. When she caught her breath and spoke, she sounded more embarrassed than anything.

'So silly,' she murmured. 'To have an accident now, of all times.'

Saffi doubted very much it was an accident. But she refrained from saying so, because just then Grandad burst in from the kitchen. He must have returned home in time to hear the crash. As soon as he saw Grandma, he blanched and hurried to her side.

'Throwing elephants downstairs again, I see,' he said.

But his face was full of concern.

'Can you move?' he asked her.

Grandma nodded. Just as he wrapped his arm around her, the clock emitted its whir and began to strike nine. It was precisely on time. Then, the sound Saffi had come to dread echoed out. The guest bell jangled.

'That's for me,' she said, rising.

'It's true,' Grandma said when Grandad started to object. 'They've asked for her. Instead of William. Because of how he is.'

That didn't please Grandad. He opened his mouth, as if to express exactly what he felt about his son and how he was. Then he thought better of it. When he turned to Saffi, there was a look on his face she hadn't seen before.

It was defeat.

'Heed rules, lass,' he told her. 'Eat nowt. Take nowt. They'll try to give Gifts. Ask for more time. Mind your Ps and Qs. They like to be called Sir, and my Lady.'

Her last sight, as she set off upstairs with the bell jingling in her ears, was of their two moon-like faces gazing up at her. Her grandparents were helpless. They couldn't stop the Lady.

10
The Lady

Room 2A, Saffi reminded herself, walking along the first-floor corridor with its green carpet. Her pulse raced as she passed a door marked *3A*, then one marked *2B*. Half of her anticipated this encounter – *finally!* – while the other half wanted to run. The lion-coat was no longer on the chair. No one else was about. Saffi stopped in front of a door at the end of the hall with the right number in polished brass. From beyond came a low murmur of voices. She reached out her hand.

But before she could knock, the door swung open of its own accord. There was a sudden hush as everyone inside looked round.

For the guest suite was full, far more so than Saffi expected. Nobody there resembled Piccola. 2A was a long room that spanned the width of the house. One side looked towards the sea, while the other faced the trees. It contained a grey velvet divan, several upholstered chairs and a dining table. On this were set out sweetmeats and desserts of every description, from chocolates and cakes to Milo's favourites, the colourful *macarons*. There was also an enormous bowl of fruit – plums, peaches, black grapes. A spicy scent hit Saffi, more pleasant than the musky smell in the hall but very strong. Somehow, though there weren't enough beds in the B&B, she guessed that there must be two dozen people in the room. A few sat but most stood about in groups of two or three.

And what people! The first comparison that sprang to mind was a costume ball. The guests were dressed in an extraordinary fashion. They wore ballgowns with elaborate wigs and headdresses, or almost nothing at all aside from rhinestones and body paint. Or were those greys, greens and golds their actual skin? They had hats, veils, cloaks of feathers; they were sequinned and bejewelled. Some walked on stilts or else the heels on their shoes were impossibly high. They hid their faces behind masks. Their clothes were made of a gauzy material like last year's leaf skeletons. Those colours, too, were shades of purple, green, grey, brown. Saffi had to make an effort not to stare at the more outlandish costumes.

'So this is the child,' said a man's voice.

On the divan at the centre of the room sat the Lord and Lady. There was no mistaking them. The Lady was the only one who went unmasked, her hair like glorious tumbleweed. With a by-now familiar shiver, Saffi recognised her as the watcher at the window, the figure in the mirror. Up close, her beauty was shocking. Saffi couldn't tear her gaze away. The Fairy Queen, if that was who she was, reclined against green cushions, facing the sea. Her dress was of the same gauzy material but white. It set off her golden-brown skin and green eyes.

The resemblance to Mum wasn't as strong as Saffi had first imagined. *Like and unlike*, she thought with a pang.

Beside her on the divan was a tall man dressed in black. At first, Saffi had the confused sense that he had a deer's head. Then she saw it was a mask and headdress, complete with antlers. His velvety brown eyes, visible through the holes, were fixed on her. He was the one who had spoken.

'Well?' he went on. 'What have you to say for yourself?'

Saffi gathered up her courage. *Ps and Qs*, she remembered.

'It's an honour to meet you, Sir,' she said. 'And my Lady. How may I help?'

The antlers tilted as he considered her. 'At least you have manners. Please,' he gestured towards the table laden with food, 'take whatever you like. We only wish to converse.'

Saffi smiled but didn't move. *Eat nowt*. The Lady was looking at her now. It was nerve-racking to be fixed on by those green eyes.

'There is one thing we require.' Her voice, low and musical, set the hairs tingling on Saffi's arms. 'The heir must speak.'

'Your father,' the Lord said, 'has declined our invitation.'

Saffi felt her heart thud in her chest. 'Ah,' she began, but had to clear her throat to go on. 'My dad isn't home, but when he's back—'

'Not him.' The Lady cut her off. 'You.'

There was a pause, as the audience watched Saffi with intense interest. Feathers quivered, rhinestones glittered. There were no more niceties. Some of the extravagant creatures crept nearer. Their scent made her dizzy.

'What do you want me to say?' she mumbled in panic.

A ripple of laughter passed through the room. 'What,' chided the Lady. But she was smiling. 'Will you not honour our agreement? We have not forgotten it. We still know who we are. What is your choice, True child?'

'Choice? Me?'

Saffi had assumed her father was the one who had to decide about the True deal. But that clearly wasn't the case. The Lord gave a faint sigh of impatience. The Lady didn't take her gaze off Saffi.

'Our offer is simple,' she said. 'For every Gift, a price. For every day, a night. Your father knew that once. Will you honour our bond?'

She waited briefly before going on. 'What do you desire, Tara Persephone? Love? Fame? Happiness?' She narrowed her eyes. 'Do you wish to belong? You are a child of two worlds. I could give you peace in one. You need no longer choose sides: father or mother, East or West. You could be at home.'

For a teetering moment it hung, clear and sharp in front of Saffi – a vision of what the Lady was offering. She had had that sense, all her life, of being torn in two. English or Iranian, foreign or local, London or Breakwell. Now, that uncomfortable duality might end. She felt like a butterfly, the Lady's gaze boring through her like a pin. This was what Grandad had warned her about. *Take nowt.*

'Please,' she said in desperation. 'Will you take your spell off Dad? I need him to see.'

The spectators whispered, a murmur like the sound of wind in dry leaves.

'Alas, your father's state is no doing of ours.' The Lady shook her head. 'Such a fate can only be chosen for oneself.'

'We gave him years,' said the Lord. 'He never came.'

'We were patient.' The Lady sighed. 'We forgave the errors of youth and love. But youth is gone. Love is gone. He remains—'

'Blind,' finished the Lord.

Love is gone, thought Saffi sadly. Somehow, the fact that Mum and Dad were together had played in his favour. That was no longer the case.

'Can nothing be done?' she asked.

'If you choose in his stead,' the Lady said, 'it will set him free. He will be as before.'

'Not that he deserves it.' The Lord snorted with disdain. 'He was blind though his wife could see. She was Sheba, he no Solomon.'

He was talking as if Mum knew about the True deal. Saffi frowned at the bright eyes behind the deer mask. It struck her, with a pang, that Dad might have helped Mum get better, if only he had believed in magic. He could have wished the cancer away. She didn't have that choice.

Did she?

'Maybe the price was too high,' she said.

At that, the Lord and Lady burst out laughing. Saffi hadn't expected this reaction and shrank back. Everyone else – all the spectators – laughed, too. The room was filled with barks, cackles, howls, hoots of mirth. It sounded like a zoo. The noise went on longer than Saffi thought possible. At last, the Lady got the better of her mirth, dabbing her eyes with a green handkerchief.

'No True ever hesitated to accept our bargain,' she observed.

'We gave them power. Riches. The world and all it contained.' The Lord's tone was cynical. 'Why stop now?'

Saffi wasn't sure what he meant. The conversation had moved on from Dad to a point about her family in general. She wished forlornly that this interview would stop. The spectators sneered at her behind their masks.

'I don't understand,' she said.

'She doesn't understand.' The Lady glanced at the Lord.

The guests shook their heads as if Saffi had committed some shameful act. It was unfair, when they were the ones who had made Grandma fall. Then she remembered Grandad's advice.

'Can I have more time?' she asked.

How it happened, she couldn't tell. She missed the steps in between. Suddenly, the Lady was close. Before Saffi could speak, she had taken hold of her chin, tilting it up so that she had to look at her. Those green eyes were piercing. They dissected Saffi's soul. But after a minute, she realised that the Lady's gaze had moved down. It was on Mum's star necklace, which had slipped out to dangle over Saffi's T-shirt. Maybe it meant something to her, for she released her hold.

'You have until midnight,' she told Saffi.

'Do not fail us,' the Lord warned as the Lady re-joined him on the divan.

It was a dismissal. They both looked away. The spectators turned their sequinned backs. But Saffi couldn't leave. A sense of injustice stirred in her. Why was she required to choose a Gift? So what if Trues had always made a bargain?

'What's the price?' she asked, almost in a whisper.

The Lady gave her a sidelong look.

'The night to your day?' she said. A smile played on her lips. 'We reveal the darkness in men's hearts, child. We don't create it. In your case, we ask a trifle: only that which is willingly given. One among you must sojourn with us, as we have sojourned here. Someone with eyes to see and a heart to know.'

Then she waved Saffi away. 'You may go. We have no further need of you.'

⚛ 11 ⚛
Questions

Saffi stumbled out of the guest suite, reeling from the revelations in room 2A. Every generation, Trues chose a fairy Gift. Every generation, they paid a price for it. It didn't seem possible to refuse. If they did – if they tried to shrug the magic off, as Dad had done – the result was disastrous. The magic moved on to the next person.

While the meeting with the Lord and Lady answered many of her questions, it left her with more. There were contradictions, too. The guests insisted on Gifts but despised those who took them. They mocked the Trues but were upset when Dad snubbed them. The Gifts weren't even proper ones, given freely. As to the price, Saffi had no idea what to make of it. She didn't trust the Lady's invitation to 'sojourn'. It might as well have been an invitation to a lion's den. Who would want that?

Now, she had until midnight to decide. It was just as well that the stairs behaved, for Saffi was too flustered to pay heed to them. On impulse, she hurried up to talk to Milo. She found him awake but still in his pyjamas, in bed.

'I've got to choose a magic Gift.' She flopped down beside him. 'Every True heir does. Dad won't, so it's me.'

'Mm-hm,' he said.

He was singularly unconcerned with the results of her meeting, after yesterday's fuss.

'Don't you want to hear about it?' she asked.

He nodded. 'Except my tummy feels funny.'

He did look pale. There were shadows under his eyes, Saffi thought. But when she touched his forehead, it wasn't hot. If Grandma hadn't fallen, she would have asked for a thermometer. As it was, they were on their own. While her brother dressed, slow and sluggish, she described her experience in room 2A. In his opinion, the Gift was 'cool'. He didn't understand her hesitation.

'I'd have chosen right away,' he said with a flash of last night's indignation.

'Something tells me there's more to it.'

'Not everything's a trick, you know,' he said.

Saffi waited while he pulled his socks on with aching slowness. Another suspicion had formed in her mind.

'You're not trying to make me stay home today, are you?' she asked. 'You know we have to meet Birdy.'

'Why?' Milo rolled his eyes. 'Can't you go on your own?'

'I suppose so,' she said. 'If someone's here.'

Later, as he dragged downstairs after her, yellow bag in tow, she wondered if someone would be. She felt abandoned by all the adults in the house. In the kitchen, they found a note on the table in Grandad's scrawl. *Took Grandma to surgery. Back soon.* Dad was still out as far as she could tell. They were stuck waiting again, this time with a fairy deadline hanging over them. Saffi was desperate to speak to Birdy; she even considered taking Milo along to his place. She supposed she might try his landline but that meant talking to Mr Lythe.

When she left Milo and went to check the study again, she saw that Dad had left his briefcase on the desk. It was open, full of papers. By now, Saffi felt a strong need to keep tabs on her father. She leafed quickly through the contents of the case. The real estate brochures were all there, along with several official-looking forms. Under those was an A4 sheet with the heading *Sopwell and Creek, Sole Agency Agreement*, which Lily Jackson had signed. The space beneath, marked 'client', was empty. Saffi crumpled up the sheet and stuffed it in her hoodie pocket. Dad could always get Lily to print another. But it made her feel better.

As she stomped back to the hall, the clock struck eleven, five minutes late. Thirteen hours remained – and she had no clue what to do about the Gift. She paced up and down in the kitchen while Milo nibbled on crackers, which was all he would eat for breakfast. Every so often, she glanced through the window but saw no sign of Grandad's red Suzuki wagon. At last, after what seemed an age, she heard the front door slam and voices in the hall. One was Dad's. She was about to hurry out to meet him when Milo spoke.

'You should ask to talk to Mum,' he said.

'You mean, as a Gift?' Saffi grasped his meaning late.

'They could do it,' he said. 'With magic.'

He didn't look her in the eye, chewing on his unappetising cracker. Of course this was what he wanted. With a stab of longing, Saffi realised she wanted it, too. Very much. But there was a catch.

'I'm not sure that's the best plan,' she said. 'How would we know it's her, not a fake? They're good at messing with us.'

He was unable to answer that.

'Let's think about it,' she went on. 'I want to try Dad again. There's got to be a way to get through to him.'

But the scene that greeted her when she hurried to the front hall made her heart sink. The musky smell was back – a harsh whiff of it, as if a fox had sprayed the place. Her father was standing in the entryway, accompanied by Lily, dressed this time in a sleek grey business suit. She was admiring the plaster moulds on the ceiling. Neither of them had registered the shifting colour schemes, the patterns on the floor tiles that wilted as Lily stepped in. It was absurd they didn't see it.

'Amazing.' Lily was gushing over the plasterwork. 'Mid-century gelatine moulds!' Then she glanced down at the puddles. 'And a burst pipe?'

'Probably.' Dad followed her in. 'Father's been trying to renovate. He does everything himself. Really, he's too old for it.'

Saffi started forward to meet them. 'Dad,' she said. 'What's going on?'

'Darling.' He smiled, cheery. 'Come say hello. This is Ms Jackson, you remember. She represents *Sopwell and Creek . . .*'

'We talked about this.' Saffi ignored Lily. 'You can't sell the house.'

'Oh, "can't" is such a silly word,' Lily said. 'Cantaloupes can't.'

She was trying to make light of it, but Saffi could see she was annoyed.

'Please forgive my daughter,' said Dad. 'My father filled her head with nonsense. Saf,' he continued, 'Ms Jackson is a visitor. Can we be civil, please?'

'You can't sell Fortune House,' Saffi insisted.

'We'll see about that.' Lily swanned past her into the hall. Roses withered under her feet. 'Your father wants to sign the agency agreement. Where did you say you'd put it, Will?'

'In the study,' he answered. 'In my briefcase.'

Saffi kept her eyes on Dad as Lily walked to the study door. She wouldn't find that sheet of paper. He worried her more: he was in a daydream, oblivious to the patterns seeping down the wallpaper. The colours changed even as she watched, from blue to grey to green. Lily, meanwhile, was having trouble opening the study door. She rattled the handle.

'What's wrong with it?' she fumed. 'It's stuck – oh!'

She forced open the door, stumbling into the study – only to stumble out again into the hall. The magic had spun her a hundred-and-eighty degrees. She stopped, baffled.

'Well I'll be,' she said.

Saffi watched as Lily turned and walked into the study again. But the door was having none of it. As soon as she stepped through to the study, she arrived in the hall. For once, Saffi wanted to cheer on the magic of the house. Lily stood there with a look on her face like curdled milk.

'Is it subsidence?' she asked Dad. 'The doors are hung at a peculiar angle.'

He was as perplexed as she was. At that moment, Saffi heard the sound she had been anticipating, a rattle of keys in the back door. Grandad was home.

'He won't like this,' she warned Dad.

Maybe Dad knew that. Saffi had never seen a grown adult look so guilty as when her grandfather strode in, without Grandma this time. Grandad stopped short when he saw Lily – the seething wallpaper – the wilted tiles.

'What's all this,' he growled.

'Now, Father, I'd like you to try and keep an open mind,' said Dad.

'Mr True.' Lily was recovering from her shock. She stepped forward with her hand out. 'Such an honour. I've always wanted to see the inside of Fortune House.'

Lily, Saffi decided, was the sort of person who didn't need fairy magic to make her ignore things she had no wish to see. Despite the business with the door, she was back to her old self, confident and smooth. Grandad pointedly did not shake hands with her. He folded his arms over his chest, scornful.

'Fiddlesticks,' he said. 'You want your commission.'

'Father,' Dad admonished.

The musky smell had grown stronger than ever. That was when Saffi saw the face. It peered down from the top of the grandfather clock and belonged to a tiny, hairy creature with a shock of ginger whiskers, much like Piccola but male. He was dressed in a mustard-coloured coat and green breeches. His fierce gaze was on Lily. But when he caught Saffi watching, he bared his teeth at her. Grandad must have seen him too, because he flinched.

Lily was unfazed. 'I can see we got off on the wrong foot, Mr True,' she said. 'Your house – it's extraordinary. I say that as an *amateur* of historical buildings. I think of it as a piece of art, not real estate.'

'Nowt for you here.' Grandad was stolid. 'Best accept it.'

The ginger fairy, Saffi noticed with alarm, had somehow hoisted a bottle almost as large as he was onto the clock, and was now dragging it towards the edge. The label read, in red letters: *Reliable Carbolic Acid*. Lily stood directly beneath as she made her sales pitch.

'The character features alone could be in a magazine,' she prattled on. 'Do you know how rare gelatine moulds in this condition are?'

Then she paused, nostrils flaring. 'Does anyone else smell that funny . . . ?'

'Watch out!' yelled Saffi, leaping forward as the bottle fell.

She ploughed into Lily, who stumbled backwards. The bottle hit the floor and smashed, splattering the tiles. Broken glass scattered all over the hall.

'What on earth?' Dad stared up at the clock. Then he turned to Grandad, accusing. 'There really is subsidence. You could've said.'

When Saffi looked again, the hairy creature was gone. Milo had come in from the kitchen and stood watching these developments with large eyes. She wasn't sure if he had seen the fairy. As to Lily, she was frantically swabbing her grey skirt with a tissue.

'This is Calvin Klein,' she protested.

The incident cut short the visit, which must have been the fairy's intent. Saffi had no doubt that he was capable of worse. Dad hurried away to fetch a dustpan and broom. Grandad steered Lily towards the front door, apologising in a way that wasn't much of an apology.

'I fear Will has lured you here on false pretences,' he said. 'This house is not for sale. Never will be. That's that.'

Lily was still peering suspiciously over her shoulder at the clock as he herded her out. Saffi heard her complaining about 'a smell of drains'. When they had gone, Milo turned to her with a serious look on his peaky face.

'I think that lady killed the tiles.'

She saw what he meant. Half the decorative tiles in the hall had gone a sickly grey, their blooms withered wherever Lily had passed. Saffi waited for Milo to leave before whispering to them. 'She's gone now.'

But the tiles remained stubbornly dead.

*

After that, the atmosphere only deteriorated between Dad and Grandad. Dad was shocked when he heard about Grandma's fall, then offended when Grandad suggested he might have prevented it if he stayed home. He stalked off to make lunch in a huff.

It wasn't a pleasant meal. Grandad was upset about Dad wanting to sell the house. Dad was upset about Grandma. Grandma called on Grandad's mobile to say that she was staying on at the surgery for scans, after which Grandad's glower was more forbidding. Saffi and Milo shovelled down forkfuls of Dad's coronation chicken and only spoke when spoken to. The one subject Saffi would have liked to discuss – the Lady's offer – was out of bounds, as Dad couldn't remember the guests.

Her father's sadness was hardest to bear. After lunch, as Saffi helped him dry dishes at the kitchen sink, he looked so miserable that she cast about for a way to cheer him up.

'It's OK,' she said. 'I don't want us to sell. I'm happy here.'

'Ironic.' Dad had his arms plunged in sudsy water. 'After all we tried to give you kids a taste of another life . . .' He broke off. 'Though she did say I'd come back,' he said, half to himself. 'That I had to.'

He was thinking of Mum. This was Saffi's chance to break through his wall of forgetfulness. 'Didn't Mum take an interest in Fortune House?' she asked. 'Like, write letters to Grandad about it?'

'Yes.' Dad's resistance must have been worn down, for he didn't even try to put her off. 'She was obsessed, if you ask me. Sir Henry, the history, the whole kit and caboodle. She had a notion that he came by his fortune in a bad way. That the family was cursed.'

'What sort of curse?' Saffi tried to mask her impatience.

He shrugged, soaping dishes. 'I honestly can't remember. Some nonsense about magic doors. I told her, it's bad enough that people like Sir Henry looted India for years. No need for curses.'

'Can I read them? Those letters, I mean?'

'I don't think I kept them.' He glanced at her. 'I cleared them all out after the funeral. There may be a couple left, I suppose. If so, your grandad has them.'

Saffi felt a spark of hope. But Dad hadn't finished.

'This old place has a way of getting its claws in you,' he sighed. 'Look what it's done to us. It's like we can't ever leave.'

After that, Saffi was convinced that there was a hidden side to the magic, something Mum had guessed. It made her even more determined to resist the Gift. She couldn't fault the fairies for hating Lily. But they had also hurt Grandma. The more she considered the question, the more her thoughts led to one inescapable conclusion.

'I'm going to end it,' she told Milo.

That was just before she left to meet Birdy. It was almost two o'clock in the afternoon. Saffi had come out on the windswept terrace to check the weather. Milo wore his blue anorak and had his yellow bag, crouched over a game of dinosaurs on the flagstones.

'End what?' he asked.

But he didn't seem much concerned, moving his line of velociraptors along. The view from the house was full of restless agitation. Clouds scudded through the sky while white-topped waves flecked the bay. Saffi kept a sharp eye on the crows that congregated in the tops of the beech trees.

'This fairy deal,' she went on to Milo in a low voice. 'There's got to be a way out of it. I'm going to ask Birdy.'

He was unimpressed. 'Why? Magic is cool.'

'Cool? What about what happened to Sir Henry?'

She glanced up at the guest suite windows again. The terrace felt exposed. There was no one looking out, however.

'He deserved what he got,' said Milo. 'Why should I care?'

It was one of his odd pronouncements. That cold, princeling air was back.

'Milo.' She gave him a hard stare. 'Did you see the fairy in the hall?'

'Which fairy?' he asked, all innocence.

She was sure that he had, now. 'They're not nice,' she warned. 'And they're not fair. They're the ones who hurt Grandma.'

'I know.'

'She didn't deserve it.'

'I know!' He looked flustered as he stood up. 'You can go without me. I don't want to see Birdy.'

'If I leave you, promise me. No talking to the guests. No going through that green door. Stay away, stay safe.'

He promised, sulky. She wondered if she could trust him. He didn't appear to grasp the danger. As she weighed up her options, Grandad poked his head out of the dining room doors.

'Going to fetch your grandma,' he said to Saffi. 'Want to come along? Might as well talk in car.'

Saffi gave Milo one last look. His expression was resentful. She wished she could read his mind. But she also knew that she had to seize her opportunity. This was the quickest and easiest way to reach Birdy. It also gave her a chance to speak to her grandfather.

'Sounds good,' she said. 'I've plans in town.'

12

Answers

As Milo steadfastly refused to accompany them, Saffi left him with Dad, under strict instructions to avoid the guests. She was glad in the end that he wasn't coming. His moods were wearing. She fetched her mac and boots, pausing by the study door to call goodbye to her father and tell him Milo was staying. Though she knew he was there, he made no reply. It didn't matter: she stepped out into the grey and windy afternoon with a sense of relief. Her grandfather waited for her in the red wagon, idling outside.

'Close call,' he said as she slid into the front seat. 'Imagine bringing an estate agent to house. Won't please the Lady.' He harrumphed. 'I expect you've got questions, lass. Since you're the heir, I'll advise best I can. How'd it go this morning?'

Now, Saffi thought, for some answers. As they drove on, Grandad nodded through her account of the meeting in room 2A. Afterwards, he went so far as to compliment her.

'I knew you'd do us proud. You've a good head on your shoulders. You don't lose your nerve. A proper True, if I may say so.'

'I wish I had longer to decide,' she said.

'Midnight on seventh day. Seems about right.'

'But it hasn't been seven days,' argued Saffi. 'They came on Tuesday.'

'Seventh day,' he said, 'is an old-fashioned name for Saturday.'

'Oh.' She hadn't known that. 'So, how does this work?' She had hoped for more information. 'The deal, I mean? What's the rules?'

They had arrived at the main junction into Breakwell. Grandad paused to look left and right before going on.

'We've a higher calling, us Trues.' He sounded stiff and important, as if making a rehearsed speech. 'This is no ordinary fairy deal. It's our job to receive the Lord and Lady when they visit this world. That's a great honour. There's rules. No eating their food. It's enchanted. Mind your manners. Don't shirk your duty. Don't sell up. Always an heir in Fortune House.'

So Birdy was right about that. 'What else?' Saffi asked.

'In return, they give Gifts. Talents, a leg up – but be careful. Don't ask for extravagances. Choose a Gift as helps all, that's best. Your forebears were inventors, businessmen, explorers. Did well for themselves and others, too.'

Saffi recalled the laughter in room 2A. Clearly, her grandfather and the Lady saw the Trues in different ways. She didn't think it was helpful to bring that up.

'What did you choose?' she said.

'A nose for a deal, that Trues may prosper.' He tapped the side of his own impressive nose. 'Suited me to stay here. I'm a country boy. I hoped to give William every advantage. Schooling, university . . . Didn't know it would turn him against us.'

Saffi doubted Dad's education was the reason for his dislike of the B&B. 'He hates the house because it worried Mum,' she said. 'Because she wrote you all those letters, back when she was sick.'

Grandad looked rueful. 'Aye. Reminds him of difficult times. Your mum knew it were important, though. She had eyes to see.'

'You mean, she saw the magic?' Saffi waited for his reaction.

'She was no fool.' He considered this. 'I'd say yes. I couldn't say owt to her, you understand, unless your dad chose his Gift. But she noticed – enough to ask questions. I wish he'd listened, if only for her sake.'

'He could have cured her?' Saffi felt her breath catch.

Grandad's eyebrows shot up. 'No, no. That's too much to ask, even for the Lady. I meant it might have made things easier. Set your mum's heart at rest.'

So the Lady had no power over life and death. She might not be able to do what Milo wanted, Saffi realised.

'He told me she wrote to you about a magic door,' she said.

'Don't know about that.' He was gruff, back to his usual self. 'It were Sir Henry she wrote about, in the main. His travels on the *White Hind*. She didn't like how he made his money. I told her what I know for a fact. Sir Henry was a cruel and ruthless man. But what he did weren't so shocking for the times, more's the pity.'

There was plenty more he wasn't telling her, thought Saffi. She would have liked to quiz him about Sir Henry. But a more urgent problem remained, that had a direct bearing on her decision tonight.

'And if I end it?' she asked. 'Cancel the deal?'

That made him frown again. 'Why *end*? It's a good thing. At least, it can be used for good.'

'What about *for every Gift a price*?'

He hemmed and hawed. He knew that phrase. 'You mean, receiving the guests at Fortune House? A bit of hard work never killed anyone.'

'There's more,' Saffi insisted. 'The Lady made it sound like an invitation. Someone to sojourn with her, she said.'

Grandad shook his head. 'She never said owt to me about an invitation. They speak in riddles, I'll give you that.'

He shut his mouth in a thin line, then, volunteering no more details. Saffi watched him out of the corner of her eye as they drove through the outskirts of town. It was strange that he could be so calm. Wasn't he worried about the price? Maybe the Lady hadn't mentioned an invitation in so many words. But he was keeping something back, Saffi was sure of it. He hadn't brought up the cave.

'And in the hall?' She hoped he would at least explain the fairy. 'That hairy creature? Who was he?'

'A sprite. Guests' help. I've often asked myself if your mum saw one. They conjure up victuals, bear messages, the like. Tricky customers if crossed. We try to keep 'em happy with cakes and whatnot.'

'Jam tarts.' Saffi understood her grandmother's endless baking.

She was still curious about the Lady's invitation, and Sir Henry. But her grandfather must have decided he had said enough, for he countered with a question of his own.

'Why so keen on this outing to town?'

Saffi was caught off guard. She didn't want to mention Birdy. 'I wanted to go for a walk, I guess,' she said. 'Clear my head.'

'That's all? Why not come with me? Your grandma'd like it.'

Saffi realised that it did come across as selfish to go off on her own. 'I just want to think for a bit,' she said, wistful.

They had pulled up on the promenade by that point. Grandad turned to face her. To her surprise, she saw sympathy in his eyes.

'Can't say as I blame you,' he replied. 'Back by teatime, so you don't worry your gran. Number fourteen bus.'

Then he fished in his jacket, handing her a phone with a cracked plastic cover. 'Any trouble, call your dad. Or the landline. We'll talk more after.'

It was as simple as that. The day was finally going her way. Saffi climbed out of the car, watching as Grandad drove off. She couldn't help feeling a giddy sense of liberation. Her watch read two-thirty, which left plenty of time to find Birdy. Dark clouds rolled in over the sea: it would most certainly rain later. But the weather held for now. As she walked down the promenade, she kept a close watch on the birds she had come to believe were the Lady's spies and enforcers. She saw nothing that struck her as out of the ordinary.

Breakwell, as Saffi knew from previous visits, had two main beaches. One was by the tea shop. Further to the south was another, fronted by ice-cream kiosks and a small fairground. This, she saw as she arrived today, had expanded. Red and yellow striped pavilions filled a lower level of the walkway, where thumping beats from a cart rink competed with the soundtrack from a Waltzer. Booths promised *prizes every time*. Looming over all, balanced precariously on its wooden frame was a big Ferris wheel, white against the cloudy sky. The glass-fronted bingo hall stood opposite. Birdy wasn't there.

Saffi chose a bench facing the sea and sat down to wait for him. Everything Grandad had told her passed through her mind as she watched the waves rush in. The fairy deal, the Gift, the price. Her watch read three o'clock, then ten past, but still Birdy didn't show. Below her, parents wrangled children with promises of candy floss. Every so often, a recorded voice from the Waltzer asked, *Are you ready?*

After a while, she rose to walk up and down the promenade. She had been waiting for more than half an hour. The rainclouds were closing in – fine pricks of moisture hit her face. Her stomach felt tight. It was unlike Birdy to break a promise. She began to fear that something had happened. Then, she saw it: a tall figure, glowering and familiar, down on the lower level of the fair. Mr Lythe strode between the rapidly emptying booths, glancing about as if he, too, were looking for his son.

He looked angry. And he was on his way to the upper promenade.

Despite Birdy's assurances that his father wasn't so bad, Saffi couldn't face his surly temper right now. She hurried away, ducking into the first shop after the bingo hall, which she had assumed sold souvenirs. Once inside, she smelled a musty paper smell and grasped she was in a second-hand bookshop. Shelves were crammed against every wall, while a row of cabinets down the middle bore signs like *Yorkshire Topography* or *Maritime Prints*. She hovered by the front display, beside an art book on a stand, peering nervously out of the window. Moments later, Mr Lythe's gloomy face bobbed by. He didn't even turn his head.

'Do you like ships?' said a voice.

Saffi gave a start. Beside her was a lady, probably the bookshop clerk – smiling, black-haired, dressed in a grey wool sweater.

'I'm sorry?' Saffi gazed at her in confusion.

The shop lady pointed to the book on the stand, which Saffi had been leafing through in an effort to look busy. The page was open at a double-page etching of a ship in full sail.

'The *White Hind*,' she said. 'Beautiful, isn't she? A Blackwall frigate under charter to the East India Company.'

Saffi stared down at the book. There was Sir Henry's ship: a long, lean, hungry-looking thing, carving its way through etched waves like a shark. She couldn't seem to escape her troublesome ancestor.

'Funny story,' the clerk continued. 'Her master was a local—'

'Sir Henry True,' Saffi breathed.

She regretted the words as soon as they passed her lips. The clerk gave an exclamation of delight, clapping her hands. The only other person in the shop – a sour-faced old man near the *Fly Fishing* section – looked up in annoyance. Saffi had been too preoccupied to notice him before.

'Don't see owt to celebrate,' he snapped. 'Cause for shame, I'd say.'

'Father.' The bookshop lady rolled her eyes. 'Don't be such a killjoy. It's nice when young people know the history.'

'Well then, tell 'em the whole tale. Start to finish,' he said. 'Tell about Sir Henry Child-Snatcher. Go on. That way she knows.'

'Please forgive my dad.' The clerk gave Saffi an apologetic smile. 'He's a bit of a history buff. But also,' she threw back at him, 'doesn't know when to stop.'

'No.' A strange sensation had come over Saffi, part excitement and part dread. 'Tell me. Why was Sir Henry a child-snatcher?'

The clerk looked increasingly uncomfortable. 'Well, love. It's just how things were done in those days. Sir Henry was what they call a "coolie master". Took plantation workers from Calcutta to Guyana. Some were very young, I'm afraid.'

'Local boys, too,' harrumphed the old man. 'Don't forget.'

Saffi felt her heart lurch. 'You mean, Sir Henry was some kind of slaver?'

'No, no.' Spots of red had appeared in the bookshop lady's face. She cast an irritated look at her father. 'They were indentures. Free after ten years.'

'Free,' spat the old man, 'if they ever arrived.'

He stared intently at Saffi. He reminded her of Grandad, scowling like that. Suddenly, she wondered if this was Birdy's 'Old Ben'. He knew enough about Sir Henry.

'It was a harsh life,' the clerk was saying. 'People didn't survive—'

'Were disappeared, you mean.' The old man gave a contemptuous snort. 'Always the young 'uns. My great-grandfather told me—'

'Dad.' The lady attempted to draw him away from Saffi. It became a gentle tussle. 'Don't take on.'

'Folks talked.' He spoke over her. 'They said—'

'Dad! She doesn't want to hear—'

'He gave them up as a tribute—'

'Your morbid stories—'

'To fairies.'

His daughter let go with an exasperated groan. 'Oh, for heaven's sake!'

There was a moment of silence. Saffi felt stuck to the floor. The old man watched her, gloating.

'I know who you are,' he said. 'You're that True lass. Daughter of William True and his snooty foreign wife. True heir always comes home.'

A customer entered the bookshop, jangling the doorbell. The sound woke Saffi from a trance. She pushed past the person, out on the promenade, feeling as if she couldn't breathe. She ignored the bookshop clerk who called after her, telling her to pay no mind to her father, that he was getting old and daft. The promenade was deserted, the rainclouds close and dark. But Saffi didn't stop, stumbling up the street.

Everything had come together for her like pieces of a puzzle. The old man might be daft but he was right. She thought of Sir Henry, ferrying all those poor boys across the world for profit. *The darkness in men's hearts.*

She thought, *we ask a trifle.*

She thought of Milo at home with their dad, who didn't believe in magic.

Now, she knew what 'sojourn' meant, and who was invited.

The Lady took children. That was her price, always had been.

13
Denial

'Where's Milo?' Saffi said, as soon as her father picked up the phone.

She had already rung him three times on Grandad's mobile, as she waited for the number fourteen bus – left two messages in growing panic, begging him to check on her brother. Afterwards, she rang the landline at the B&B, but no one picked up. Finally, on the third try, Dad answered with a harried voice.

'Saffi? Isn't this your grandfather's phone?'

'He lent it to me. Where's Milo? Have you seen him?'

'Isn't he with you?'

Saffi's chest felt tight. Her dad thought Milo was with her all this time. He hadn't heard her, or hadn't paid attention to her call through the door before she left. She didn't know if that was fairy magic or pure bad luck.

'Dad!' she cried. 'I told you I was going out alone.'

'You need to make your plans clear. It's OK. I'm sure he's upstairs, watching a film. Why so upset?'

He wouldn't understand any reference to magic, so she couldn't say. 'Is Grandad home yet?' she asked.

'Not yet. Are you all right? Do you need a ride?'

The bus, Saffi saw was approaching. 'Bus is here,' she said. 'I'll be back soon. Please, can you check on Milo?'

'Sure.' He seemed amused. 'Never pegged you for a mama hen.'

She wanted to yell down the phone that he needed to be more of a daddy hen. But it was pointless.

'Bye, Dad. I'll call after you've checked.'

But he didn't answer when she called back, as they were crawling on at a snail's pace through the town. Saffi wanted to throw Grandad's phone out of the bus but could only wait, chewing on her dread and frustration, while they meandered through what felt like every single side street in Breakwell. When they reached the main road, the driver was kind enough to show her the right stop for the B&B, near the *No Horses* sign. After that was another long, anxious walk down the lane. Dad still wasn't picking up.

By the time she arrived at the house, the rain was coming down, a steady downpour that made puddles on the gravel drive. She was glad to see Grandad's wagon parked beside Dad's Skoda. So everyone was home. As she stepped into the hall, the grandfather clock struck five, its chimes preceded by the usual hiccupping sound as if the mechanism was stuck. The tiles were still a mournful black and grey.

'Milo?' she called, leaving her mac in the entryway.

No one answered. The study door was open, so she

checked there first. It was empty. When she peered into the dining room, she noticed all the doors of the display cabinets were open. She could see Milo's yellow backpack through the French windows, lying on the rain-soaked terrace. He wouldn't be playing outside in this weather. After that, she checked the living room and kitchen, calling her brother's name. She even poked her head into the basement.

By this point, fear clutched at her belly, accompanied by a horrible, twisting sense of guilt. She should never have left Milo. Her instinct had told her something was off. She hastened to the hall, intending to check the upstairs bedrooms. There, she met her grandparents coming down. Grandma's right foot was in a blue cast. She took each step slowly, clutching the banister; Grandad had one arm wrapped around her waist, holding a pair of crutches in his other hand. Saffi gazed at them both askance, wondering how much they knew about the Lady's price.

'Why the hullabaloo, love?' Grandma asked. 'We heard you all the way up in bedrooms.'

Dad walked in from the kitchen. 'And in the yard,' he remarked. 'What's going on?'

'Milo's in danger,' Saffi said. 'Has anyone seen him?'

'Not lately, lass.' Grandad frown deepened.

'What d'you mean, danger?' Grandma winced, leaning on her crutches.

'Those guests want to take him.' Saffi kept her eyes on Grandad. 'That's their price. They take people. Did you know?'

Grandma was evidently horrified. Grandad looked more troubled than shocked by the news, but shook his head.

'No,' he objected. 'That can't be right.'

'You're obsessed with these guests, aren't you?' Dad said.

Saffi glared at him. Maybe her grandparents weren't aware of the Lady's intent, but Dad's denials were too much.

'I told you to check,' she burst out. 'First you think he's with me, then you think it's all in my head. You've no idea if he's in the house!'

Grandma appealed to him. 'Is this true, William?'

Dad was about to answer. Then he hesitated, staring at Saffi as if in doubt. He didn't remember their telephone call. She wanted to scream. Grandma's face had drained of all colour. She whispered something to Grandad, who helped her sit down on one of the hall chairs. Saffi rounded on her father again. It was easier to be angry with him than think about how bad she felt for leaving Milo.

'Why didn't you believe?' she cried, no longer caring if he understood. 'Why didn't you at least try to go upstairs?'

Dad glanced at the other grown-ups, as if he expected Grandad and Grandma to shrug off whatever his daughter was talking about. When they were silent, he became bewildered. Grandma was too upset to speak.

'Don't seem right.' Even Grandad looked shaken. 'There's rules, though your father displeased them. We have until midnight . . .'

But as he mentioned rules, Saffi remembered the Lady's

comment. *Nothing that is not willingly given.* She hadn't stolen Milo. She didn't need to.

He was all too ready to go.

'It's him, not them,' she said. 'Milo. He thinks he's found Mum . . . Long story,' she went on when the others were baffled. 'I know where he is. He's gone to the sea caves.'

She hurried towards the entryway. 'Care to explain?' Dad followed. 'I've heard about some guests, a Lady, caves . . . I'm a little lost.'

'He had this vision.' She grabbed her mac, pulling it on. 'A door to heaven. I bet you anything he's gone back there. I'll find him.'

'But it's high tide,' Grandma protested. 'You can't.'

'Not alone.' Grandad moved to unhook his own raincoat.

'Saffi,' said Dad. 'I don't know what this is all about, but a beach trip is just silly at this time of day.'

Saffi made no answer, zipping up the mac. Grandad turned to Grandma. 'Best someone stays,' he told her.

'Not much else I can do,' she replied with irritation.

'Are we actually indulging her?' Dad asked.

But Saffi was already striding out of the door. The rain had eased but the wind blew strong. She heard Grandad's voice from behind, then her dad's. She ignored them, slithering down the slope through wet grass. All her guilt and worry had crystallised into one driving thought. She would find Milo. Stop him. Bring him home.

When she reached the steps, she saw what Grandma meant. The beach below the B&B was gone. Grey, foamy water rushed up to the ramp, swilling between rocks. A strip of stones remained but she wasn't sure if it continued to the point. There was no one in sight, no Milo. She climbed down anyway, gripping the handrail, the wind stinging her cheeks. At the end of the ramp, she paused to stare out at the waves – huge ones by the bluffs, sending up spray. She doubted she could pass.

Her father and grandfather had started after her by then, Grandad's dark mac flapping like wings on the stairs. Saffi could hear them calling. But she wanted to at least try to get to the point. She set off along the last bit of beach. It was hard going. She struggled on, sliding and stumbling on wet stones. The cliffs towered above, and she found herself remembering Birdy's warning about walking too close. Now, she had no choice. To her right, the foam hissed up to her toes.

Halfway around the bay, she was forced to a halt. Ahead of her, grey water swilled against the cliffs. She searched for a path through and found none.

'Milo,' she whispered in despair.

Then something odd happened. As she stood by the rushing waves, she could have sworn she heard Birdy's flute. She strained her ears for the sound. Again, the sweet-sad notes drifted on the wind. She flinched as Grandad's fingers clamped down on her arm.

'What's got into you, lass?' he yelled over the crash of waves. 'Can't go that way. Have to use top paths. Why make us come down?'

He obviously heard no music. Saffi didn't try to free herself. A listless, hopeless feeling had come over her. The sea had won. The Lady had won. Dad had caught up to them now. Before he could tell her off, she flung herself into his arms, burying her face in his chest.

'Hey,' he said, holding her. 'It's OK. It's all right. Let's get back, we're not going to find him like this.'

It was a subdued Saffi who trailed after her father and grandfather, back up the slope to the house. She listened to the grown-ups debating what to do. Grandad wanted to check the top paths, while Dad was keen on calling the coastguards and police. As to Saffi, she was certain that Milo had gone to the cave, not the cliffs. Birdy might have been there, too, if her ears hadn't tricked her. Had he seen Milo? But her father and grandfather were too deep in their discussion to listen to her suggestions. She followed them up to the rain-blackened terrace.

There, a flash of yellow gave her pause. Milo's pack was still lying out on the flagstones. No one had brought it in. Saffi had an overwhelming urge to touch it, as if doing so might bring him back. But when she went to pick it up, she caught a whiff of a delicious smell from inside. She opened the flap with a sense of misgiving. Jumbled among brontosauruses and velociraptors were several pink and green *macarons*. The last time she had seen similar ones, they were on a silver cake stand in room 2A.

Milo had eaten the food from the pantry. Saffi dropped

the bag like a hot coal, hurrying after her father and grandfather.

'He took it,' she panted as she caught up. 'The food. It was in his bag.'

'What food?' Dad was uncomprehending.

But Grandad understood. His face grew pained. 'How long's this been going on, lass? When did he start?'

Saffi could only shake her head. Questions crowded her mind. When had Milo taken the fairy food? Today? Yesterday? She remembered his moodiness, the stomach ache. She could have kicked herself.

'All right, tell me what I'm missing,' said Dad.

'Dad.' Saffi willed herself to be patient. 'Our guests – yes, the ones upstairs – come from another world. It sounds crazy but it's true. They've taken Milo.'

'I'm afraid she's right, Will,' said Grandad.

Dad opened his mouth to laugh, or argue, then stopped. He rubbed his hands over his face, a troubled look in his eyes. Saffi wondered if he was starting to remember. Maybe magic was like that, a gradual ebb and flow of realities.

'Another world,' he murmured.

'No point checking cliff paths.' Grandad had a grim look, opening up the front door. 'If he's et their food, he's with 'em now.'

Grandma was waiting for them in the hall. She struggled to her feet with the aid of her crutches, her face speaking her question.

'No,' was Grandad's response.

'So you're saying these guests want to kidnap Milo?' Dad had finally accepted the fact of their existence.

'Oh dear.' Grandma glanced from one to the other.

'Like as not, he wanted to go.' Grandad's answers were curt.

Dad's gaze was full of horrified astonishment. Saffi could tell that some inkling of the truth had dawned on him, and with it, fear.

'I've been a fool,' he said.

'Where are you going?' Grandma asked. 'Will?'

For he had set off, abruptly purposeful, striding past them towards the stairwell. He didn't even take off his coat and boots.

'Get my son back.' He marched up the stairs.

'That's not the way,' Grandad called. 'There's rules. Can't just barge in!'

'William.' Grandma hobbled after him with Grandad's help, shuffling up the steps. 'Don't do anything stupid.'

But Dad didn't answer, disappearing around the stair return. Her grandparents followed, their faces full of anxiety. Saffi was about to hurry after them when she saw something else.

At the top of the grandfather clock, the glass door that protected the clockface was ajar. Inside, plain as day, balancing with one foot on the minute hand and the other on the number three, was the red-haired sprite. No one had noticed him. As she watched, he reached up clawed fingers to move the picture wheel, rotating it until it showed the castle in daylight. Once that was done, he climbed off the clock hands, slid down the beading on the wooden case and hopped to the floor. Glancing at Saffi, he gave a broad wink and tapped his nose like Grandad. Then, he was gone.

Saffi shook off her torpor and followed her grandparents, at a loss as to what she had witnessed. Whatever the sprite was doing, it would have to wait. On the landing, she found the green door wide open. Beyond it, the door at the end of the corridor was also open. Grandma and Grandad stood outside. Dad's silhouette was visible inside the guest parlour. He was speaking to someone.

'. . . who you are,' he was saying. 'But I won't let you take my son.'

The parlour, Saffi realised when she approached, was almost empty. The flamboyant audience of earlier on had disappeared. The only guests present were the Lord and Lady. The Lady sat on the divan, gazing out of the open window. She didn't seem to mind the rain blowing in. The Lord was on his feet facing Dad. Saffi hadn't grasped just how tall he was until then. His antler headdress brushed the ceiling, so that he had to bend his head. Saffi felt Grandma's hand on her arm, pulling her back. Her grandparents watched with anguished eyes but didn't enter.

'You will speak to my Lady in a manner befitting,' said the Lord.

His voice crackled at the edges, not quite human. Saffi's skin crawled. She heard a rumble of thunder from outside, smelled the odour of electricity in the air. The storm was closing in. *Get away!* she wanted to shout at Dad. Instead, he faced up to the magical creatures before him – brave or stupid, she was unable to tell.

'Answer me,' he said. 'Where's Milo?'

'Will, please . . .' Grandma murmured.

He didn't look at her. Then the Lady spoke.

'We have not yet had the pleasure of an audience with you, William True.' She didn't take her eyes from the window. 'Now, you accuse us of reneging on our agreement. No harm has come to your son, I assure you.'

'So tell me,' he begged. 'Whoever you are. I'm sorry I didn't believe. Where is he?'

Saffi heard the catch in his voice. But something more was happening outside. Over the choppy sea, a funnel had begun to form in the clouds. As she watched with dread and fascination, the tail of it stretched down to the water like a silver snake. It moved towards the cliffs in total silence.

'Dad,' she said. He ignored her.

'Your son is safe,' answered the Lady.

'You stole him,' Dad burst out. 'That's not safe. You've no right!'

'Enough!' thundered the Lord. 'You go too far.'

A gust of wind blew the windows wide open, splattering wet leaves. Saffi saw in amazement that snowflakes whirled outside. Snow in August. The snake-like plume of water was approaching the cliffs. But Dad never noticed it, or else he was too desperate to care.

The Lady had stood up in the meantime, her white dress like a pale flame in the gloom. Her gaze was fixed on Dad.

'I have every right,' she said.

The atmosphere in the room was green, swamp-like. Saffi wanted to yell at her father to run. But her tongue sat heavy and useless in her mouth.

'You see now,' the Lady continued. 'Don't you?'

Dad, Saffi realised now, was watching their guest with the most peculiar expression. She had expected him to be angry or afraid. Instead, his face was full of wonder – or maybe a sudden, terrible hope. He took a step towards the Lady. The funnel was so close to the window that Saffi could taste the salt spray.

'Perhaps,' the Lady's voice was gentle, 'you wish to join your son.'

Saffi heard Grandma's gasp. Then, lightning and thunder struck together with a deafening clap and blinding flash. The storm beat down with renewed fury, sending the windows banging open. Leaves and even a few twigs swirled through the air. Downstairs, a door slammed. Saffi must have blinked, because when she looked up, the room was empty.

The Lord, the Lady and Dad had vanished. The room was empty. There was no sign of a cloud funnel outside, nothing but the wind and the grey-white sea.

14
Breach

Saffi stared in horror at the place on the rug, drenched with water, where her father had been. She had already lost Milo. Now, she had lost Dad, too. The memory of his eager expression haunted her. Had he wanted to go with the Lady?

Someone pushed past her into the room. Grandma hobbled in on her crutches, glaring at her husband.

'Henry.' Saffi saw a rare flash of anger in her grandmother's eyes. 'Tell me right now. Where's William? Where's my son?'

Grandad had followed her, to glance in a dejected way at the leaf-strewn furniture and waterlogged rug. He shut the window.

'He's in breach of contract,' he said heavily. 'Shouldn't have barged in . . .'

'Barged, pish.' Grandma was beside herself. Saffi had never seen her so furious. 'I've put up with this tomfoolery long enough. Creatures from I don't know where, staying days on end for I don't know what reason, requiring heaven and earth . . . I did everything they asked. Everything. They still took my boys.'

'I warned you when we were married. This is Fortune House. They visit.'

'You said, *maybe once or twice in a lifetime.* You said, *don't worry, our family's safe.* Do you feel safe, Henry?'

Grandad gave her a helpless look. Saffi shook off her stupor. Grandma wasn't the only one with questions. It was time to set the record straight.

'Grandad,' she said. 'Were Dad and Milo taken as the Lady's price?'

'Poppycock.' He scowled at this. 'It's William's fault. If he'd taken his duty seriously, none of this would have happened.'

'What about Sir Henry?' she pressed. 'Was he the only one who sent children away as a tribute, or were there others?'

'Those are vicious rumours. People say all sorts.'

'So you don't know,' she said.

He gazed at her, irritated. It was Grandma who spoke up in her defence.

'She has a point, Henry. Listen,' she went on as her husband huffed with annoyance. 'What about those other vanishings, over the years? Great Uncle Jack? Aunt Moira? There's always been something off with this family. I think Anoush was right.'

'If so, it weren't on purpose,' he objected. 'Not a tribute.'

Grandma was counting on her fingers. 'Your second

148

cousin, Ethel. They said she fell off a boat in Cairo, remember? Uncle Jack: lost at sea. Little Jimmy: anaphylactic shock. No one saw it. Cremated, no remains. Aunt Moira: met a boy and emigrated to America. Emigrated? Really? At fifteen?'

'I expect some people were curious and went where they weren't supposed to.' Grandad sighed. 'Yes, fine, Aunt Moira. But it was an accident.'

'The accident,' Grandma said, 'is by design. It's part of the price.'

He had no answer to that accusation. Saffi went to stand by her grandmother, slipping an arm through hers. They faced Grandad together.

'So?' she asked him. 'What'll it be? Trues or the truth?'

He opened his mouth to argue. But even he must have had his doubts, for he closed it again and frowned. Grandma drew herself up, leaning on Saffi.

'Henry William True. You're to find a way to bring my boys back from wherever they are. Or God help me, I'll not speak to you again.'

'That makes two of us,' added Saffi.

Grandad had no hope against this united front. 'Well, of course,' he spluttered. 'What d'you take me for? I have to think. Give me a minute.'

He looked more than a little lost to Saffi. But she had heard enough to give her a glimmer of hope.

'So there's a way to go after them?' she asked Grandad.

'Yes. Maybe. It's difficult.'

'There's a way.' Grandma wasn't going to let her husband off the hook. 'He can use the True door. He's done it before.'

'The cave?' Saffi did a rapid calculation. 'I guess tides are low at midnight . . .'

'Not a cave.' Grandma had her eye on Grandad. 'At Fortune House.'

Saffi recalled Mum's letters about a magic door. All this time, she had thought it was the fissure in the cave. But there was another way into the fairy world. She listened closely as Grandad answered.

'That's a gamble and you know it. William won't even remember who he is by the time I find him. Most likely, neither will I.'

Saffi didn't waste a moment longer. 'I'll do it,' she said. 'I'll go.'

'Not you, love. It's dangerous.' Grandma gave Grandad a pointed stare.

He turned to Saffi, awkward. 'Fairy world steals your memories,' he explained. 'Especially if you're taken there sudden, like your dad. Even with precautions, it's risky. Can't stay or eat the food. You'll forget why you came. Forget your own name.'

Saffi understood. The Lady's invitation was a death sentence.

'So.' She tried to hide how frightened she was. 'You know where to find them. You have a door. But you won't go in, because it's risky.' He started to speak but she carried on. 'I was wrong to blame Dad. You're the coward.'

Grandad looked sad rather than angry. 'You've never been there,' was all he said.

Just then, frustratingly, the landline jangled downstairs. It only rang when someone needed a booking at the B&B. Grandad turned to go.

'We did look for poor Moira,' he remarked before he left. 'One hour, we managed. Miracle we made it back at all.'

When he was gone, Grandma pulled Saffi close in a hug. 'He'll do it,' she assured her. 'He'll go after them. Don't fret.'

'Fine,' said Saffi. 'I'll go with him.'

'You'll not.' Grandma was fierce. 'I can't lose you as well. Help me downstairs, love. Ankle's killing me.'

Saffi had no intention of letting her grandfather search for Dad and Milo alone. She was ready to return to the cave if need be. For now, though, she helped Grandma downstairs. Grandad was still on the phone as they arrived, pacing up and down in the study, so angry with whoever it was that he only barked a word or two at a time. It was past seven, Saffi saw with surprise when she checked the clock. Two hours had flown by. The image of the castle was back to its night position.

All at once, Grandad slammed the phone down and strode out of the study, eyebrows bristling at Saffi. 'Have you been consorting with Lythes?' he said.

When she had no answer – she wasn't sure what 'consorting' was but it sounded biblical – he pointed to the phone. 'That Thomas Lythe just called. Seems he met you under false pretences. Is that so?'

'I made friends with Birdy.' She opted for the truth. As far as she was concerned, she had done nothing wrong. 'He knows who I am.'

'Well, your so-called friend's missing.' Grandad harrumphed. 'Took Milo down to sea caves, or that's what his father thinks. Never came back. He makes enquiries, finds out from Ben Wishaw – of all people! – who you are. Calls me to say, and I quote: *If you've done owt to my flesh and blood, Henry True, I'll come for you and that skinny bint, too.* Just so you know what type of folk you call friends.'

'Birdy took him to the cave?' Saffi couldn't fathom this. 'Why?'

'Give it a rest, Henry,' said Grandma.

'She shouldn't make friends with a Lythe,' Grandad almost shouted.

'But why'd he take him, and not say?'

Saffi still didn't understand. Birdy hadn't met her when he said he would. Instead, according to his father, he had been with Milo. She even heard his flute.

Grandad's face was full of angry triumph. 'I wonder who's stealing children now.'

'But Birdy wouldn't!' Saffi cried as she grasped his meaning.

'Wake up, lass,' he said. 'How d'you know he doesn't have his own arrangement with the Lady? I imagine that lad could do with a fairy Gift.'

Saffi quite hated him in that instant. The look on his face reminded her of Milo in his worst moods – cold and superior. Birdy was her friend. He wouldn't do such a thing.

Would he?

'Of all things to say, Henry,' Grandma chided.

'I need some air.' Saffi's throat was tight again. She could hardly get the words out. 'I'm going for a walk. I won't be long.'

In the face of Grandma's protests that it was too late, that it would soon be dark, she grabbed her mac and stepped outside. She had no particular destination in mind. Her grandparents didn't follow, thankfully. Behind her, she heard Grandma telling Grandad off, calling him a *daft apeth*. Their voices faded as she walked down to the cliffs for a second time that evening. It had stopped raining. Fog lay over the bay but it was still light.

Saffi felt empty, hollowed out. It was horrible. Everything was horrible. Halfway down the slope, she halted to gaze at the sea. The rain had beaten the grass on the clifftop flat, like fur on the back of a vast beast. The sound of waves was muffled. Dark thoughts filled her mind. Was it possible that Birdy had betrayed her? She wished she had never met him, never trusted him. She wished she hadn't left Milo. Most of all, she wished she still had Mum. She wouldn't have let this happen. Saffi's hand crept up to the star pendant.

Then, with a surge of furious anger, she yanked it off, cast it away. So much for a way home.

She stood staring out at the foggy bay for a long time before turning to go back. But she didn't get far. Every step dragged as if she had weights on her legs. Finally, she gave in and hurried back to rummage through the wet grass. The stems were broken and matted. It was several breathless seconds before she found the pendant, glinting among the roots. She fumbled with the catch to put it on. Luckily, it wasn't broken. She hesitated in the gathering twilight, unsure of what to do next.

At that moment, a voice spoke. It came from a dark clump of trees to Saffi's left and almost made her jump out of her skin.

'Saffi?'

It was Birdy. She saw him better when he stepped away from the trees. He had come to find her. Without pausing to think, she rushed up to him, raining blows on his chest with the flat of her hand.

'How could you! How could you! I trusted you!' she cried.

He fell back in the face of her fury, looking shocked. 'Steady up.'

When she struck him again – admittedly not very hard – he caught her wrist. 'Whoa. Enough.'

Birdy wasn't much taller than her, but he was wiry and strong. He wouldn't release her wrist until she had stopped flailing and stood still. Then he let go and took a step back. His face was a pale blotch in the foggy evening light. His hair was wet, jeans soaked through as if he had been caught in the rain.

'Listen—' he began before she interrupted.

'Did you take Milo to the cave today?'

'Take? No—'

She cut him off again. 'The Lady stole my dad.' As he gazed at her, speechless, she continued. 'Milo, too. So tell me. Where were you this afternoon?'

'Top paths,' he replied. 'By Beacon Hill. I've been trying to say. I saw Milo.'

'I thought you said you didn't take him.'

'Saw. From up top, OK? He was on beach. With someone – I didn't see who.'

She had to ask. 'Did you talk to him?'

'Didn't hear me. It's high, no stairs till South Landing. It were either follow and see where he goes, or meet you. So I followed. He went back to that cave all right. After that, I came back to tell you. No need to act crazy.'

But he looked more worried than annoyed, rubbing his eyes. 'Flippin' 'eck,' he sighed. 'Should've known it would end like this.'

'Why's that?' she said, sarcastic. 'Because you knew they'd take him?'

He didn't answer. But the comment found its mark, she could tell. She went on accusingly. 'You knew they'd steal Milo. That's why you pulled him back in the cave the first time. I don't know what you think you're doing, Birdy. But it looks like you're playing both sides.'

'I only suspected,' he insisted, 'after it happened.'

When he didn't go on, gazing miserably at her, she folded her arms. 'If you don't tell me what you know, right now, we'll fight. You'll win but I'll fight. Is that what you want?'

'No.'

'So, say it.'

He took a ragged, unhappy breath. 'It's not first time Lady's been seen in that cave,' he admitted. 'First time was me. I didn't know who she was then.'

'You better tell the whole story from the start,' said Saffi. 'Then you'd better explain why you didn't tell it days ago.'

She could see that it was difficult for him to answer. He couldn't meet her eye. When he did speak, staring out at the final dregs of red sunset under the clouds, he sounded more clipped and Yorkshire-ish than ever.

'It were maybe three years ago. Those days, Mum still lived with us. Her and Dad were always having a go. Just shouting,' he added. 'But I hated it. One day, I couldn't bide things at home. So I ran down to cave. That's where she found me.'

'The Lady?'

He nodded. 'So beautiful, I thought I was dreaming. Comes to sit by me. Says, *Would you like your mum to be happy?* What could I say but *yes*? In my mind, that meant with Dad and me. But after, Mum got a job in Scarborough. Wouldn't change it, I guess.'

He turned to look at Saffi, earnest. 'The Lady never asked me for owt, I swear. I only realised later – that I might put you and Milo in danger. I was daft to take you to that cave.'

She wondered whether she could ever believe him. He had suspected what was going on but hadn't told them, aside from his vague warnings about the guests.

'Please don't be mad,' he begged. 'I'd never hurt you, never in a million years. Not even for her. I want—'

Even as he broke off, Saffi felt the change in the air. Birdy looked up, then hastily threw up his arms. She watched in horror as dark shapes bore down on him, filling the sky with whirring wings. The birds came in droves – seagulls, crows, jays, dozens of smaller ones Saffi couldn't identify. They flew at his face with single-minded purpose, beaks and claws outstretched. All he could do was cower down on the ground with his arms over his head.

At last, she understood. This wasn't just magic that didn't want to be talked about. This was a punishment. Birdy had chosen them over the Lady.

Saffi didn't hesitate. Peeling off her mac and twisting it up into a tight looped rope with both hands, she made a whip to beat the birds off. She laid into them repeatedly until they rose up again, screeching. Even the seagulls retreated.

'Get off him!' she shouted. 'I have until midnight. The Lady gave me till midnight. You leave us alone, you hear?'

Maybe they understood her, because they stopped flying at Birdy's head. For several minutes, they wheeled above the cliffs, giving their raucous cries. Then, as quickly as they had come, they went. There was only the darkened sky and fog rolling in on the breeze.

Birdy rose slowly to his feet, brushing flecks of white off his jacket and jeans. Saffi realised they were downy feathers.

'I was saying,' he resumed, 'I want to protect you.' He gave a wry laugh. 'Except, I'm thinking you don't need it.'

Saffi knew she had a choice, then. It was simple. Her choice was to believe him or not. If she believed, everything he had done would be explained, and they could work out the rest together. If she didn't, she would have to say goodbye and never speak to him again.

'Come on,' she said. 'Let's get out of the weather.'

15
A Plan

'So you were in the fields at six?' Saffi said.

She and Birdy had walked back to the house, to sit down on a bench under Grandma's lilac arbour. It was sheltered enough that Saffi felt protected from the birds, but not quite inside yet. She wanted to get every detail out of Birdy before they confronted Grandad. He obliged her by repeating his account of Milo, including the strange way the tides behaved at four-thirty in the afternoon, lying all the way out on the rocks. After that, he had tried to return to the B&B, only to be caught in a storm and forced to shelter in an abandoned bunker until it passed.

'Snow, in August,' he said. 'Never seen such a thing.'

Saffi was satisfied with his account. It agreed with what she had observed from the guest suite – the snowflakes whirling. Only her timing question remained.

'Because if so,' she went on as he nodded, 'why'd I hear a flute on the beach?'

He opened his jacket to show her the ripped lining inside. The flute was gone. 'Weren't me,' he said. 'I lost it in the storm.'

'I'm sorry,' Saffi said. She knew how much he loved it.

But she felt relieved, her heart lighter. He had chosen them over the Lady. The birds' fury was proof enough of that. That was why they were so hard on him: they considered him a traitor. Saffi couldn't help speculating what it would mean for his mother. Whether it would undo the magic that gave her a new life. She didn't dare ask.

That, of course, brought them to tonight's problem and the midnight deadline. Briefly, she told Birdy about Milo's disastrous choices and the possibility of a True door.

'Thing is, Grandad won't say where it is, or how to use it,' she finished. 'He doesn't want me going in with him.'

Birdy shrugged. 'Maybe he won't mind if it's me.'

'Not alone,' she said flatly. 'Anyway, he thinks you're some kind of felon who took Milo. I'm not sure how to change his mind.'

'We tell the truth.'

They could only try, Saffi supposed. 'The fairy world is dangerous,' she said after a minute. 'Are you sure you want to help?'

She peered in his face. The evening light was almost gone, the sky a deep grey-blue. Her grandparents had switched on the living room lamps, blurred rectangles of yellow. Her question to Birdy had more riding on it than she cared to admit. She needed an ally.

His cheeky grin was the most heartening thing she had seen all day.

'Just try and stop me,' he said.

So the matter was settled. But as they rose to go, Saffi heard the landline again, a dim summons from the house. She pulled Birdy behind the arbour. Watching through the study windows, she saw Grandad come in, followed by Grandma on her crutches.

It seemed to Saffi that whoever was calling had bad news. She imagined it might be the police, someone Mr Lythe had involved. Grandad didn't talk for long. He was even grimmer than usual when he hung up and spoke to Grandma. Their conversation was inaudible but Grandma looked pale. Grandad helped her to the hall, switching the lights off. Then, the front door slammed. Saffi realised in surprise that they were leaving. If she didn't hurry, she would miss them. But Grandad was in a terrible rush. By the time she and Birdy walked to the front of the house, he was in the car with Grandma.

Saffi watched the wagon pull away on the drive, wondering where her grandparents were headed at this hour. Surely they knew Milo wasn't likely to be found by the police? At the same time, this was an opportunity. Grandad would have left the back entrance unlocked for her.

'Come on,' she told Birdy. 'Let's find that fairy door.'

Soon, she was letting him inside, turning on the kitchen and hall lights, feeling like a thief in her own home. Unfortunately, they had very little to go on in their search. They knew only that the True door was somewhere in the house. But Saffi felt they had encountered magic enough times to look for patterns. Wherever fairies passed, the surroundings were affected. The cave flooded, tiles and wallpaper changed, stairs stretched or shrank. Perhaps if they looked carefully enough, they might find another sign.

She was also fairly sure where to start. The guests had come upstairs on that first night. If they had arrived by a magic portal, chances were it was on the ground floor. Birdy agreed.

'Upstairs was rebuilt after the fire,' he said. 'Downstairs stayed the same. Makes sense that magic's there.'

The wallpaper in the hall was back to its usual yellow-green tonight, the tiles to red and white. But Saffi wasn't duped. There was still a whiff of the musky odour she associated with sprites. They searched the study first, where she hoped to recover one or two of Mum's letters. All they found stuffed in the desk drawers were tax receipts. After that, they tried the dining and living rooms, with no better luck. Saffi was sure that at least half the ornaments were missing. The fairy food had vanished, the pantry shelves bare of all but crackers and sardines. A brief tour of the bedrooms confirmed that these were non-magical zones. As to the guest suite, she was by no means certain it was empty, and thought it best to steer clear.

It was getting late by then, long past dinnertime. Saffi expected her grandparents home at any moment. Finally, distracted by hunger, they made a quick meal of sausage rolls and apples in the kitchen. After that, they returned to the hall. All was still and silent without a scrap of magic in sight: the grandfather clock ticked on towards ten. Saffi bit her lip with annoyance.

'Let's go over this again,' Birdy said. 'Where've you seen these guests? If anyone knows where that door is, it's them.'

'The hall.' She reeled off a list, counting on her fingers. 'The upstairs suite. But they only took Dad that way because he broke the rules. Also, the pantry.'

'Can't imagine Fairy Queen coming in by a pantry,' said Birdy.

'Shhh.' Saffi placed a hand on his arm. 'Was that a laugh?'

She could have sworn she heard the disembodied chuckle again. But when they listened, there was only a renewed patter of rain. The musky whiff was faint.

'Saf.' Birdy had walked to the foot of the stairs. 'Is that your mum?'

Saffi realised the photos were back. With all the other upheavals that afternoon, she had forgotten about this fairy prank.

'My gran takes them down, for Dad's sake,' she said. 'But someone always puts them up again. I don't know why.'

Birdy moved up a step. 'Wow, your mum's a looker. Sorry,' he amended. 'I mean, she's beautiful.'

'She was a looker,' said Saffi sadly.

The photo he had commented on was a black-and-white one of Mum standing in front of the grandfather clock. Saffi had to ask herself what she would have made of the events at the B&B. In the photo, Mum was wearing the star necklace;

Saffi was grateful, reaching up to touch that reassuring shape at her throat, that she hadn't left it on the cliffs.

She saw something else, too, one difference between the past and now. In the photograph, the picture wheel on the clock showed the castle in daylight. The mechanism had been working then.

'I forgot.' She turned to Birdy in excitement. 'I saw a sprite inside the clock. Before they took Dad. He changed that picture wheel from night to day.'

They both rushed over to the grandfather clock. Birdy opened the glass cover.

'He just spun it,' said Saffi.

She could smell the works inside, the bitter tang of brass and oil. The second hand ticked on, while the inscription on the disc was easier to see with the door open. *And there was no more sea.* Birdy was tall enough to reach the wheel. He was careful to use the tips of his fingers to avoid the moving parts on the clock, easing it first in one direction then another. After a few tries, he withdrew his hand.

'It's stuck,' he said. 'I'm afraid I'll break it.'

Saffi's stomach fizzed with impatience. She was sure they were close to an answer. 'We can't fit in it, can we?' she asked.

But even when she turned sideways, the space at the base of the clock was too narrow to serve as a door.

'I wonder what that means,' said Birdy. '*No more sea.*'

Just then, the buzzer sounded at the front entrance – a loud, long ring, making them both jump. They stared at each other in bewilderment.

'Who on earth?' breathed Saffi.

She hadn't noticed a car drawing up on the drive, too preoccupied by their search. As she stood there, frozen with indecision, she heard a shrill barking from outside. Someone pushed open the letter slot to call through the gap.

'I know you're there, Saffi. Open up, please.'

It was Lily, of all people. And she had brought her awful dog.

⟫ 16 ⟪
A Problem

When Saffi went with great reluctance to open the door, she found herself face to face with her neighbour once again – this time a vision in a pale pink cocktail dress. Lily looked as if she had been to the sort of boring adult party where everyone drank champagne and talked about real estate. At her feet was Treasure, idiotic as ever. He trotted in as soon as the door opened, nails clicking on the tiles.

'I heard about Milo,' she said to Saffi, breezing in without an invitation like her dog. 'I came to see if—'

But as she laid eyes on Birdy, she stopped short. 'Whole town's out looking for you, Birdy Lythe!' she exclaimed. 'They've got coastguards, a red alert . . . we thought you were lost with the True lad.'

'My dad called coastguards? For me?'

A spasm of alarm crossed Birdy's face, as if the prospect of his father's concern was worse than his anger. The poodle had gone over to sniff at the base of the grandfather clock. He gave a shrill little yap.

'Shush, Treasure,' said Lily.

The dog whined. Lily took out a silver phone from her purse. 'Is your dad off with the search?' she asked Saffi, keying in a number.

Saffi decided it was better just to nod, at a loss as to how they would look for magic doors with Lily in the house. Treasure could no longer contain himself and yapped again.

'Hush, darling.' Lily frowned at Saffi. 'Do you have rats? Really, the amount of hidden issues in these old places . . . Hello, Steven,' she continued in a bright voice, as someone on the other end picked up.

'He's going to kill me,' muttered Birdy when she had turned away.

Saffi guessed he meant his father. 'D'you want to phone him?' she whispered.

'Best not.'

Treasure had got wind of something in the clock, jumping up and yapping with wild excitement. Lily placed her finger in her ear.

'At Fortune House. I know,' she said after a minute, strolling away, 'but he is. So you can call that search off.'

Saffi sidled over to Birdy. 'Why not?' she asked.

'Because this is all my fault.' Birdy was dismal. 'I said I'd take Milo to caves. To make my dad happy. You don't know how he is.' He lowered his voice in a gruff impression of Mr Lythe. '*You'll not walk out with some chit from London.* I said, *It's the lad, he wants fossils.*'

'Ah,' said Saffi in dismay. 'That's a bit messy.'

'Just a bit. Now everyone thinks it's my fault Milo's gone.'

Lily was nodding on the phone, wandering down the hall. Treasure lost interest in the clock and trotted over to sniff at the chair. Saffi watched with some concern as he picked up the doorstopper figurine in his teeth, slinking off to a corner with it. She didn't care for the statues but supposed her grandparents would.

'Hey,' she hissed at the dog. 'Put that down!'

The absurd creature growled as if he was guarding a bone.

'True child,' said a dry little voice. 'You ought to be ashamed.'

It came from inside the clock. Saffi looked round to see the familiar red-haired sprite, ensconced this time in the lower section where the weights hung. He had cracked open the door to peep out, whiskers bristling. Birdy gawped at him in surprise.

'Is that what I think it is?' he asked.

'Tell yon hellhound to unhand me wife!' spat the sprite.

Treasure growled again. Lily looked up from the far end of the hall. 'Could you switch off that tablet or whatever?' she called. 'I can't hear myself think.'

'What's he mean, *his wife*?' Birdy whispered when she turned away again. 'What's Treasure got that he's so upset about?'

Saffi didn't move, her eye on the sprite. 'An ornament. There's loads in the dining room.'

'You should know better,' the sprite scolded. 'Your brother saw!'

Saffi knew that the sprites obeyed the Lady. But right now she was ready to wring this one's hairy little neck.

'What d'you do to Milo?' she said.

'Nowt!' the fairy answered roundly. 'Only he'd eyes in head, unlike some.'

'As far as I know,' Lily said, switching the phone to her other ear. Then, after a silence: 'I don't know, watching a film or something.'

'Piccola.' The sprite gazed in anguish at Treasure. 'My love!'

'Piccola?'

All at once, Saffi had a qualm. She went over to look at the statue. Birdy followed. The dog tried to hide his prize from them both. Saffi waited for Lily to look away, then pounced.

'Give it back,' she said, wrestling the statue out of his mouth. 'Let go, you stupid thing.'

She wrenched the figurine loose, giving the dog a look so severe that he cowered. Then, she examined the statue. It was one of the animal-head ornaments, less repulsive than many of its fellows, with a pleasant if weasely little face. Apart from being covered in drool, it was intact. The figure clasped its front paws together and was dressed – only now did Saffi see the resemblance – in a ruffled gown.

With belated understanding, she saw what Milo must have seen, long before she did. 'Piccola,' she said.

As she spoke the name, a change came over the statue. She heard Birdy gasp in amazement as the hard wood became soft brown skin, the carved hairs red fur and the dress, wet through, a cotton forget-me-not print. Piccola sat up in Saffi's palm, gazing at herself in disgust.

'Slobbered all over,' she sniffed, as if this were the worst fate imaginable.

Saffi placed a finger to her lips in a plea for silence, slipping the sprite into her mac pocket just before Lily turned around.

'Let her go!' shrieked the sprite in the clock.

'Eh?' Lily was saying. 'Right then. Yes. Right.'

Saffi could see Piccola's curious face peeping out from beneath the pocket flap as their visitor ended her call.

'Someone's on their way.' Lily put the phone in her bag. 'I offered to drop you off, Birdy, but my friend says best let coastguards do it.'

Maybe she expected Birdy to be grateful, but he only fixed her with his steady gaze, hands in pockets. Saffi knew that the last thing he wanted was to be at home with his dad. Lily looked affronted.

'Well,' she said. 'I suppose I can stay a while. Keep an eye on things.' She smiled but the smile didn't reach her eyes. 'Just till Mr True comes home.'

Saffi balked at this. 'I'm sure he doesn't want you to wait up late.'

At that moment, several things happened. Treasure, divested of his prize, had gone back to the clock. He must have seen the sprite for just as Saffi mentioned lateness, he leaped up with a volley of ear-splitting yaps, slamming himself against the casing. The sprite tumbled onto the floor, right at Lily's feet. She stared at him for a frozen second before he scrambled up and hurried away. Treasure tore off in pursuit, barking madly. Both raced around the corner to the kitchen.

'Oh dear,' gasped Piccola in Saffi's pocket.

Lily stared down the hall after them for a long, aching instant. At last, she spoke. 'Do you have a cat in this house?'

Saffi had an idea. There was a kind of desperation in Lily's face, a need for easy explanations that could work in their favour.

'I'll sort it out,' she said soothingly, taking her visitor by the arm. 'Why don't you go wait in the living room? I'll make tea.'

'I'll help.' Birdy had caught her eye, understanding.

It was a calculated risk. Saffi was relying on Lily's desire for normalcy – her blindness, as the Lord would put it – to shield them from questions about the ginger blur. Something similar had occurred after her run-in with the study door. She needed to believe she was in control. The hunch turned out to be correct. Lily allowed herself to be led to the living room, silent and meek. Saffi's last sight was of her sitting down in Grandma's green chair. There was a haunted look on her face, as if the children, the B&B and everything in it were puzzles she hadn't figured out yet.

Saffi left her to it, and made for the kitchen with Birdy.

The scene that greeted them was comical. The red-haired sprite danced on the chequered tablecloth, eyes bulging with indignation. He had thrown whatever came to hand at his nemesis: a salt cellar and one of Grandma's spatulas lay on the floor. Now he shook his fist at Treasure, who cowered under the table.

'Fiend!' he cried. 'Brute! Hellion! Wife-killer!'

'What are they?' Birdy was watching Piccola. 'Some kind of fairy?'

Saffi lifted the lady sprite out of her pocket, to set her gently down on the kitchen table. Treasure growled but didn't intervene.

'Sprites,' she said. 'Servants to the Lady.'

'Scoundrels!' The male one was spluttering. 'Unfit to bear the True name—'

'Oh hush, Mr B,' Piccola told him. 'Stop your roaring. I'm fine.'

He shut his mouth like a trap when she spoke. 'I didn't know she was your wife,' Saffi said in an attempt to mollify.

Mr B gave her a hard stare. 'Did the beast maul you?' he whispered to Piccola. 'Did it torture you?'

Treasure gave a final yap. 'As you can see,' Piccola said with disgust, 'it slobbered me.'

'Birdy.' Saffi remembered her *Ps and Qs*. 'This is Piccola. Piccola, Birdy.'

'Stop gawking, boy,' said Piccola. 'Where are your manners?'

'I apologise.' Birdy recollected himself and made a bow, hand on heart. 'Honoured to meet you.'

'The honour is mine.' Piccola gave a prim nod. 'This is my husband, Mr B.'

The male sprite bared his teeth.

'Piccola.' Saffi had a sense of precious time slipping by. 'We're in trouble. Could you help us?'

'Of course.' The end of the lady sprite's nose twitched. 'How shall we curse that blonde harridan? Foot odour?' Her face lit up. 'A love potion! Whoever she sees first tomorrow shall be her true love. The postman, the garbage man . . .'

Birdy couldn't suppress a snort of laughter.

'It's not about Lily,' Saffi said. 'It's my father. And brother.'

'Has Mr True made peace with my Lady?'

Piccola looked genuinely concerned. Perhaps the sprites weren't aware of what happened in the house while in their statue state.

'A Royal Sanction, more like,' grunted Mr B.

'Oh. I'm sorry to hear that.' Piccola's face fell.

'He was taken,' Saffi explained. 'I have to find him in the other world. I need you to tell me how to open the True door. Please, Piccola.'

The request made the sprites uneasy. Mr B took a step back, as if the question might attack him. Piccola looked torn. Birdy watched them closely.

'I'd be delighted, if you chose a Gift,' Piccola said. 'But going against a Royal Sanction – it's high treason. My Lady would be most displeased.'

'I can't take that Gift. If I do, I might never get Dad and Milo back.' Saffi held her gaze. 'But if you could do anything . . . They're my family. It's a small one, but it's all I've got.'

Piccola's black eyes were huge as she appealed to Mr B.

'I can't bear it,' she murmured. 'Poor, motherless creature. Can't we help?'

'My dove,' he replied, 'Her Royal Highness will have our 'eds. One word about that door and we're nowt but dust and ashes.'

Under the table, Treasure gave a pathetic whine. Piccola reflected a moment.

'Then we shall speak of other things. I wanted to tell you, young Saffi. You remind me of your mother. Such a lovely lady.' She glanced at her husband, who was kicking at the tablecloth with very bad grace. 'I particularly like those pictures of her in the hall. Can't think why they keep taking them down. I like to put them up again.'

Mr B glared at her in furious silence.

'Didn't she give you that pretty necklace?' Piccola remarked to Saffi in a breezy way.

She lifted one clawed finger to tap her chest, her eyes on the star pendant. Saffi's pulse quickened. This was a clue.

'Yes. She said it would guide me home.'

'And so it shall.' Piccola beamed. 'The lodestar will lead you aright.'

It was Birdy who leaned over to whisper the answer in Saffi's ear.

'That photo of your mum wearing the necklace. She's by the clock. Has to be important.'

Saffi agreed. Before they could do anything about it, however, the kitchen door burst open and in came Lily. Panicked, Saffi darted a look at Piccola and Mr B; to her relief, they were both gone. Only two quaint statues stood on a shelf above the table. Lily's doubts had also vanished. She fixed her eyes on Birdy, brandishing her phone.

'You,' she accused him. 'You were seen out on cliff paths today. What were you doing up there? Were you with the True boy or not?'

She didn't even use Milo's name. Birdy's face had acquired the wary closed look it had when he was with his dad. He said nothing.

'He was on his way to meet me,' said Saffi.

'All afternoon?' Lily gaze bore into Birdy. 'He was seen twice, hours apart. And he can answer for himself, can't he?'

Saffi wondered if people here had nothing better to do than monitor their field paths. But when Birdy stayed stubbornly silent, she felt obliged to speak.

'He saw Milo. He came to warn us. What's it to you?'

'What it is, young lady,' said Lily with a haughty smile, 'is that I'm the responsible adult in this house. Your father would want me to find out.'

Saffi highly doubted that. But Lily's insistence on her own version of reality was now a problem. She had convinced herself that Birdy was guilty.

'Out with it, boy,' she snapped. 'Did you take Milo to the caves?'

'I'll talk,' said Birdy with quiet dignity, 'when I'm listened to.'

'You've got the wrong end of the stick,' Saffi told Lily. 'He just saw him.'

'I can't believe you're defending him,' Lily sneered. 'Are you that stupid? Why wouldn't he go home to get help if he saw your brother out alone?'

'Because—' began Saffi.

But a swift look from Birdy stopped her before she mentioned Mr Lythe, or the kiosk. He had no wish to tell Lily about his family issues. She couldn't blame him.

'He had nothing to do with Milo's disappearance,' she finished lamely, before realising too late that she sounded guilty herself.

Lily looked from one to the other. 'I see,' she said. 'He made a foolish mistake and ran to you for help. You're protecting him. That's what happened.'

'It's not, though.'

But Lily kept on. 'He's been hiding here. Don't lie to me.'

'I'm telling you the truth,' cried Saffi in fury.

Treasure during this time had cowered further under the table, agitated by the tone of the debate. Now, he began to whimper. Lily was intent on Birdy.

'That's for the police to decide,' she said. 'And believe me, I've made sure they will. Detective Inspector's on her way.'

She seemed about to go but paused. 'If you two were thinking of slipping off,' she went on sweetly, 'it'll be worse for you. Now, I could do with that tea.'

After that, she marched out of the kitchen, followed by a cringing Treasure. When they were gone, two small figures hopped down from the shelf.

'I've not seen such wilful folly in all my years,' Piccola

said. 'A love potion is too good for her. She shall have horrors. Nightmares. Cramps!'

'Piles,' added Mr B with a wicked grin.

'I can't believe she called the police.' Saffi gazed worriedly at Birdy.

'Changes nowt,' he said.

But she could tell that he was upset. He hid it by going to put on the kettle. 'You check the clock again,' he told Saffi. 'I'll make tea.'

'We can do that, dearie.' Piccola arrived on the stovetop, quick as lightning, before he lugged the kettle back. 'You do whatever you need to do.'

'You're sure?' Birdy asked in surprise.

'She shall have the best brew in Yorkshire.' The lady sprite beckoned in an imperious way to her husband.

'Thank you,' Saffi called to them as she hurried away with Birdy.

Glancing over her shoulder in the doorway, she caught sight of the two sprites bent over the firebox as Mr B blew life into some kindling. She wasn't entirely convinced she could trust them. But she had no choice. Midnight was fast approaching. If they were going to find anything before running afoul of both the Lady's deadline and the police, they would have to do it soon.

17

Hope

'Where, though?' Saffi murmured to Birdy.

They were standing in the hall, speaking in whispers as Lily was visible through the double doors to the living room. Saffi was sure that Mum must have hidden something in the clock, maybe her letters. They had looked behind it. Then under it. Then on top of it. They even opened the casing and looked inside, where the sprite had been. But there was no sign of anything unusual. Birdy was about to reply when Lily's voice rang out.

'I'm not sure why tea takes so long,' she said. 'D'you pick it in China?'

Birdy gestured to Saffi to wait, calling over his shoulder as he headed back to the kitchen. 'Just brewing!'

When he left, Saffi looked up at the clock again. 'Where are you, Mum?' she sighed.

As if in answer, the clock hiccupped and struck eleven. It was almost right, Saffi saw, checking her watch. Only an hour remained until midnight. At that point, it occurred to her that the mechanism might be making its odd noise for a reason. She opened the casing again, frowning up at the images on the clockface. The lion seemed familiar to her, as if she had seen the design before. There was a painted sun behind it. The stars above the castle on the island were shaped just like Saffi's pendant. A snake, she noticed, twisted in the grass at the boy's feet. She felt as if the answer was just out of reach. Finally, she stuck her face inside the lower casing, to peer up at the brass cogs behind.

And then, with a lurch of hope, she saw it. A wad of paper – no, a thick envelope, pale blue. Stuffed behind the cogs.

A letter! No wonder the wheel wouldn't turn. Saffi tried to pull it out but it was wedged tight. The teeth on the cogs were clamped down. As she tugged, a corner of blue came off. Dreading to lose the rest inside the mechanism, she worked it out, millimetre by millimetre. It took all her patience. At last, she had the envelope in her hand. It contained several pages of blue stationery, somewhat mangled by the cog. With trembling fingers, she slid out the first, covered in her mother's neat cursive script.

My very dear Saffi, it began.

Saffi's vision swam so she couldn't read on. The letter was addressed to *her*. She had somehow expected it to be part of Mum's correspondence with Grandad. But why would she hide that in the clock? Grandad hadn't told her what she wanted to know. Dad didn't believe her. This was her personal message to Saffi.

In the living room, Birdy offered Lily a tray of tea and

biscuits. Saffi couldn't bear to read Mum's words with her bothersome neighbour in her line of sight. She hurried back to the kitchen. There, seated at the table, she took the pages out one by one, laying the blue squares reverently on the chequered cloth.

My very dear Saffi. I am writing this because I know that one day, you'll need it. Your dear dad doesn't want to be bothered with Fortune House. He says the past is the past. But I suspect you'll grapple with its legacy, as I have. It's part of who you are. Not the only part – which is why you might see a way out. You know how to be two things at the same time, even two very different things. It isn't always comfortable but it is useful. Listen to that feeling. I believe it will help you.

Stay uncomfortable.

Since I can't ask your dad to give you these notes, I've left them under the sign of our star. I've reason to think they will find their way to you. By then, I hope, you'll be grown up.

Saffi glanced at the top of the letter: it was dated from two years ago. So much for Mum's hopes. But her heart hammered as she continued reading. It was like hearing her mother's voice again, her soft accent in her ear.

The story begins when one of your ancestors, Sir Henry True, chose to enrich himself through the

suffering of others. I want to say that before anything
else, because I believe that's what cursed him. Greed is
the rock this house is built on. Magic was only a
means to an end . . .

Saffi read through the rest, three pages' worth, then read it again, because it didn't feel as if it had sunk in the first time. The True deal – the magic door – it was all there. Mum had written about the whole sorry business, from Sir Henry's choices to the fairy price, though she didn't have any firm answers about how to end the deal. While she was still lost in the letter, Birdy came back in with a brooding look on his face. Lily must have said something to displease him. But he grasped that Saffi had made an important find and sat down to wait for her. At last, she looked up.

'Mum wrote this for me,' she said. Her voice was hoarse.

'I sort of guessed.'

He pointed to her face. Saffi realised her cheeks were wet. She brushed the tears away.

'Right.' She took a deep breath. 'There's lots here that's useful. Mum did a bunch of research on history and legends. She spoke to Old Ben, too, but doesn't agree with him. She insists Sir Henry was the one who suggested a tribute. That's how he thought the bargain worked. Let's see . . . *He proposed a tithe of souls in return for 'wishes three'. One of his wishes was to have Fortune House with its magic door. I suppose he thought he was being cunning – that he'd get more Gifts* that way. Instead, he lost everything. Wife, peace of mind, sanity . . . The family hushed it up.'

Birdy gave a low whistle. 'So he tried to burn the place down.'

'He had regrets,' said Saffi. 'A bit late. Listen to this. *I do not know whether to call these beings who come and go to the house evil. Sir Henry tried to control them. Your grandad wants to appease them. Their Queen, I think, has her own idea of right and wrong. Sir Henry traded in bound labour. We shouldn't be surprised if his legacy binds us . . .*'

Birdy was leaning close to her to peer at the page, tracing Mum's handwriting with his finger. 'The way she writes – it's kind of like a book of legends,' he said. 'You wouldn't know she's foreign.'

'Birdy,' said Saffi in exasperation. 'She lived in England half her life. Went to school and uni here.'

'Sorry.' He blushed. 'I'm daft. Does she talk about a True door?'

'It has to do with the clock and the mirror. She thinks they work together like some kind of machine. She even drew pictures.'

Saffi turned to another page, to show him Mum's pen and ink sketches of the clockface with its four illumined figures, the carved oak leaf pattern on the mirror. '*Clock and mirror were made by fairy craftsmen,*' she read. '*They work as one, if you have the key. I imagine that's handed down as part of the True legacy. According to tales, the door opens at midnight. I myself have heard footsteps downstairs, though your grandparents will admit to no visitors. Travellers must return before the twelfth chime . . .'*

She puzzled over that. 'I don't understand how we can get there and back inside of twelve chimes.'

'*True legacy.*' Birdy squinted at the writing. 'Which is?'

'No clue. There's not much else. A bit about how the deal works.' Saffi frowned over the last section of the letter. '*Fairy contracts are written in intentions, not ink. There's no piece of paper. But I believe such deals are a test. Maybe that's how we end it. We approach them in a different spirit.*'

The final lines were hard for Saffi. She swallowed before going on. '*This is the last time I will visit Fortune House. I've done what I can. The rest is up to you. You are stronger than you think, Tara, my little star. Be wise – be brave – be who you are.*'

She blinked away the mist in her eyes. 'So,' she said after a minute. 'We want to get Dad and Milo. What about all those other people Sir Henry tricked? Is it too late for them?'

Birdy never answered her. Their gaze met as they both heard a sound – one Saffi had been dreading since Lily announced her plans. From outside the kitchen window came the unmistakeable crunch of wheels on gravel.

They scrambled to their feet, staring at each other in panic.

'Quick,' said Saffi. 'What's this legacy? Any ideas?'

'Money?' Birdy threw out suggestions. 'Land?'

'Something that makes the clock and mirror work together. A key.'

'What else did Sir Henry leave?' Birdy's eyes had strayed to the windows. Lights were flashing blue and red outside. 'Pictures? Things? Furniture?'

'Yes. Those statues!'

It made perfect sense once Saffi saw it. She had even heard Grandma using the term to describe the ornaments: *family legacy*. She was about to rush off to the hall, fired up by this possibility, when Birdy grabbed her arm.

'And if it works?' he said. 'What about the forgetting?'

Saffi had relayed her grandfather's warnings. Luckily, she had already given some thought to the problem. 'We'll need a reminder.'

She found the permanent marker Grandma used for labels on jars. Frowning with haste – outside, car doors slammed – she wrote messages on each of her palms. On her left, she marked *get Dad and Milo*; on the right *no food*. She did the same for Birdy, except that on his left she wrote *get Saffi's family* and on the right *no food*.

'This might work,' he said, staring down at his hands.

The messages made Saffi consider something else. On the off-chance that they would find themselves in another world, she retrieved more sausage rolls from the fridge and placed them in a cloth bag, along with Mum's letter. She didn't want to be parted from it. After that, they both went back to the hall.

There, however, Saffi's courage almost failed her. The front door was standing open. Lily must have gone out to meet the police, because a squad car with flashing lights stood on the drive. A dim babble of voices rose up. Saffi forced herself to ignore them, aware that time was running out. It was ten to midnight. She went to inspect the clock and mirror, racking her brains as to how they worked.

'Notice how they're hung opposite each other?' she whispered to Birdy. 'The leaf designs even match up.'

'Except at corners,' he said.

It was true. Where the mirror had decorative alcoves in each corner, the oak leaf and acorn designs on the clock continued, unbroken. The alcoves, moreover, were oddly shaped. They didn't match each other, let alone the clock.

'It has to be four ornaments.' Saffi was sure of it. 'One that's made to fit each alcove.'

But before they could test out the theory, a low beam of headlamps shone through the door as another car arrived. Glancing outside, Saffi saw four vehicles: the police car, Grandad's wagon, Lily's mini, and now a muddy pickup truck. A knot of people stood by the police car. Grandad was there, scowling in his usual way. Grandma leaned on his arm. One of the police officers was holding Milo's blue anorak. Lily spoke with expansive gestures as Mr Lythe emerged from the truck. No one was looking in their direction. As soft as she was able, Saffi pushed the front door to, until she heard a satisfying click. It wouldn't keep Grandad out, but might delay Lily.

'Didn't you say there were more of those statues?' asked Birdy.

They had to hurry, as it was five to midnight now. But in

185

the dining room, another hurdle awaited. Though the cabinet shelves were half-empty, there were still far more than four items.

'Which ones?' Saffi groaned.

Outside, someone rang the front door buzzer. She could hear voices: Lily saying something about 'sneaky so-and-sos', Grandad protesting. There was no time to try each ornament in the mirror. Even as she reached out to grab one at random, Birdy bent over one of the shelves.

'Your Mum's sketches,' he said. 'Wasn't there a lad?'

He pointed out a bronze figure of a snake charmer, a cobra at his feet. Saffi understood.

'Yes.' She snatched up the statue. 'We need the ornaments that match the clock. Swan, lion, whale.'

The buzzer rang again, loud and long this time, while someone hammered at the door. Saffi and Birdy each chose a cabinet to go through.

'Whale,' Saffi breathed in triumph, holding up a bone carving.

'Hello?' A woman's voice called through the letter slot. Her tone made Saffi think it was one of the police officers. 'Is anyone home?'

'I'll open up,' came Grandad's voice. 'Let me through.'

'D'you see a lion?' Saffi peered anxiously at the figurines. There was a horse and an ox, but nothing like a lion.

'No,' said Birdy from his corner. 'No swan, either. Unless . . .' he picked up a carved jade piece with wings outstretched. 'Some kind of bird, anyway.'

Saffi heard the sound of Grandad's key rattling in the lock. He was having trouble opening it. She wondered if that was fairy magic, too, working in their favour for once. She combed the shelves, fearing at any instant to hear clock chimes.

'Let me in,' thundered a voice. Saffi recognised Mr Lythe. 'They've got my son in there!'

'Stuff and nonsense,' Grandad shouted. 'Your boy took Milo!'

'For goodness' sake,' Lily said. 'The kids are stalling.'

'Come on, come on,' Saffi muttered.

The malachite mask stared back at her, inscrutable. Birdy joined her at the right-hand cabinet to help look for the lion. Then, the sound she had been anxiously awaiting echoed out from the hall. A chime, light and sweet.

The first stroke of midnight.

'What about that coin?' said Birdy at the same time.

It was a large silver one on a stand, inscribed with an image of a lion and the sun. Saffi suddenly remembered where she had seen that image before, in Mum's books. It was the symbol of Persian kings. The second chime rang out as she snatched it up – a third echoed while she and Birdy scrambled back to the hall. At the same time, Grandad won his tussle with the door. Saffi saw a ruffled forget-me-not blur leap away as it opened. So Piccola had helped them. Behind her grandfather were several people, all elbowing past each other to get in. The police officer was calling for calm. A fourth and fifth chime sounded while Saffi and Birdy fumbled figurines into mirror alcoves, trying them in different places to see what fit. The coin had an obvious home, a slot on the bottom right. Birdy also found a spot for the swan, top left, shaped for upraised wings.

Grandad meanwhile was shouting that it was his house, so he ought to be the first inside. Mr Lythe said over his dead body. No one listened to the police officers. Treasure was madly yapping. The sixth and seventh chimes struck while Saffi and Birdy tried to make the whale and the boy fit in all the wrong ways, before understanding that the whale went upright at the bottom and the boy at an angle at the top. Birdy's father must have seen him, for he bellowed out his name. People crowded through the entryway. Dim and far-off, the eighth chime struck. Saffi expected Grandad or someone to grab her by the arm.

Instead, as the snake-charmer slotted into place, curls of grey smoke rose up from the surface of the mirror. Then there was no glass, just mist in the frame. A gust of spray hit Saffi as if they were beside the ocean. Someone took hold of her hand but it was only Birdy. Beyond him, to her right, was a strange sight. The hall milled with people but they were moving too slowly. Some were frozen in place. The interval was long between the chimes; the ninth hadn't yet sounded. Voices rose up in a groaning cacophony. Mr Lythe loomed large behind his son. The mirror frame was as big as a door, or else the two of them had shrunk. Water splashed in from an invisible sea.

'Shall we?' Birdy asked. He was the only one who looked normal to her.

'Together,' said Saffi.

Hand in hand, they stepped through another burst of spray into the mirror, just as the ninth chime rang out.

18
Forfeit

The chime deepened until it was as loud and sonorous as a church bell, a deep long boom that shook Saffi to her core. After it ended, the echoes faded away, leaving a dim ringing in her ears. There was no sign of the mirror. She was standing with Birdy in a vast tidal basin at low tide. Ribbed brown sand stretched away in all directions, reflecting slices of blue. In a disconcerting shift, it was daytime on the other side of the door. The sky was suffused with afternoon light.

In front of them was a scene she recognised at once: a craggy island surmounted by a house made of pale stone. It wasn't fortified enough to be a proper castle, dotted with too many windows. It was, of course, the same as the one pictured on the clock. Island and house were the only features on the tidal plane, aside from a few jagged boulders on the shining sand. Sunlight turned the windows bright gold.

'*And there was no more sea*,' murmured Saffi. She realised that she was still holding Birdy's hand and let go in embarrassment.

'Aye.' He glanced about. 'And won't stay that way. Fresh puddles, see?'

Now, Saffi knew where the water tracked into the hall at home came from. The stillness and silence were extreme, though she could just imagine the waves rushing across the sand at high tide.

'Well.' She roused herself. 'I suppose we ought to get on.'

A shell-strewn beach lay at the foot of the crags, some five hundred feet distant. From there, a path wound up to a postern gate. Dad and Milo had to be in the house. There was nowhere else. She was about set out when Birdy spoke.

'How do we talk to them? Do we have a plan?'

Saffi had been too caught up with the business of finding the door to think of anything else. But her feelings on the subject were clear.

'About time someone ends this cursed deal,' she said. 'There must be a way.'

Would the Lady laugh if she sued for mercy, she wondered? Appealing to Piccola was one thing. This was entirely different. At the back of her mind was the idea: *At worst, I can offer myself in exchange for Dad and Milo.*

'Bet you it won't be easy.' Birdy was frowning up at the house. 'You saw what happened with your dad. Can't just walk in and make demands. There's the forgetting magic. How do we remember we have those messages on our hands?'

He was right again. Though the writing was on her palms when Saffi checked, she hadn't remembered it in a while.

'I know,' he said. 'Let's hold hands again. That way, if we

forget what's what, we'll wonder why and look down. Then we'll see.'

It had the virtue of being simple. Saffi took hold of his. Aware that time was passing in this world, however differently, they set off for the island. But they hadn't gone more than a dozen steps before they stopped, disorientated. The island was further away than ever.

'First snag,' said Birdy.

Then, Saffi remembered Lily at the study. 'Hang on,' she said. 'Let's try something.'

She deliberately put her back to the island and set off in the other direction, pulling Birdy along. In the blink of an eye, it was before them again. Now it drew nearer.

'Right laugh, this place,' said Birdy. 'Everything upside down.'

'Mirror logic.' Saffi smiled.

As they walked on, she guessed this would be only the first of many surprises. There wasn't a breath of wind in the bay, which somehow made her nervous. The rib-like trenches in the sand were deeper than she first thought, too. Like her sense of direction, her size judgements were off: everything was bigger than she expected. The house towered over them, more ominous with every step. It seemed to change shape gradually, revealing hidden parts of itself until it no longer resembled the one on the clock. Those shining windows might conceal a thousand eyes.

At the jagged rocks, Birdy stopped. 'Someone's following,' he whispered.

He beckoned Saffi behind one of the boulders. After a while, she heard a patter of feet, someone splashing through puddles. A minute later, an astonishing creature came into view. It had the lower body and legs of a large dog with a skinny human neck and head, topped by a cherubic mass of green curls. The fur on its body was also light green. It craned its head left and right as if looking for something; its bug-eyed features were vaguely familiar to Saffi. Otherwise, it was the ugliest creature she had ever encountered, more comical than threatening. Without waiting for Birdy, she stepped out to confront it.

'Who are you and why are you following us?' she demanded.

The fairy being danced back on the sand, looking so silly that Saffi almost laughed, before remembering. *Manners.*

'I meant no harm,' it replied in a snuffling, nasal voice. 'Name's Figment. I was curious. We don't often see visitors here.'

'We won't be here long,' said Birdy.

Saffi chose to be polite. 'I'm Saffi. This is Birdy,' she said. 'Pleased to meet you.'

Figment gazed at her with open curiosity. He took a step closer.

'Are you bound for Forfeit House?' he asked.

'You mean the castle?' Saffi couldn't help peering up at it.

'My Lady's domain.' Figment sounded cheerful, as if he was talking about a walk in the park. 'So-called, because all who enter forfeit their hopes and dreams.'

'Charming,' said Birdy under his breath.

'We still have ours,' Saffi answered. 'And we intend to keep them.'

She was beginning to think they were wasting precious time with Figment. His bug-eyed face was full of bland stupidity.

'So exciting!' He took another step forward. 'We haven't had hopeful visitors for ages. The last time I saw Hope in my Lady's house, it flew into one of the windows and knocked itself clean dead. Feathers everywhere. Terrible shame.'

Saffi saw that his eyes were fixed on the bag containing the sausage rolls. So that was what he wanted.

'I'm sorry, but we have to get going,' she told him. 'We don't have much time.'

She started to move off but the fairy being followed.

'Are you just going to walk straight in there?' He snuffled at the odour from her bag. 'Because your hopes won't last long that way.'

Saffi glanced at Birdy, who shrugged. 'Why?' she said.

'Front door's enchanted. Step in and bam! All your memories go.' Figment grinned happily. 'You'll want the back door. Much better.'

It was a ploy, Saffi could tell. But it might also have been true. She looked hard at him.

'And you can show us?'

'Oh yes.' Figment gave a sideways hop of excitement. 'I ask only one thing in return.' He wet his lips. 'I'm so hungry,' he whimpered. 'If you've a bite to spare . . . anything . . . Proper victuals are hard to come by in these lands.'

Again, Saffi had a sense that she had seen this behaviour before. The way he watched her hand as she reached into the bag was distinctly canine. It reminded her – yes, she was sure of it – of Treasure. Was that even possible? In any case, once she saw the resemblance, she couldn't ignore it. Even his voice was a breathless bark.

'Ank you, ank you.' He kept his mouth wide open as he spoke, dancing with excitement. 'Ust 'ro it in.'

He had no arms, so she had to lean gingerly forward to slip the pastry between his yellowed incisors. As soon as he had it, he jerked his head back and gulped down.

'Oh my,' he mumbled, cheeks bulging. 'So good.'

Then he set off across the sands, looking self-important. 'You coming?'

There was no direction-switching this time. As they hurried after Figment, the craggy sides of the island drew close. They were near enough now to see that the place was lifeless. No trees or flowers grew in the castle courtyards, not even grass. Despite Figment's story of Hope, no birds or other living things moved on the bluffs. There was only stone, sand, shells, glass. As the sun dipped gradually towards the horizon, a line of shadow from one buttress inched up the walls. Its stark bare beauty struck Saffi as joyless. She was haunted by the thought of her dad and Milo trapped in that dreary edifice.

Figment, in the meantime, was making a wide circuit around the island. 'Why do you wish to visit my Lady?' he asked. 'Sorry to be inquisitive. Like I say, we don't see many folk.'

'I want to find my father and brother,' Saffi said.

She looked behind her in a reflexive way, fearing to see the incoming glint of the tide. But for now, there was nothing visible on the horizon.

'Are they visiting too?' Figment chattered on. 'It used to be different here, you know. People coming and going all the time. Kings and queens . . . Prince Pwyll and his dogs . . . King Solomon himself.' He gave Saffi an inane grin. 'Is your father a king?'

It was Birdy who replied when Saffi was silent, sick at heart. 'They've been taken,' he told Figment. 'They're prisoners.'

'Oh,' said their guide. His expression grew more sympathetic. 'I see. So you'll be throwing yourselves on our Lady's mercy. I wish you the best, I really do.'

A few moments later, as if he couldn't help himself, he added: 'Not that she's known for her mercy.'

'Would you convince her for us?' asked Saffi.

Figment gave her a panicked look and quickened his pace. 'Me? Good grief, no. I'm just a go-between.'

'Any advice, then?' Saffi called as they followed.

At least the request for help had made him hurry up. He veered off to the left, eager to reach the island now.

'Don't eat the food,' he said. 'Those in Forfeit House eat their own dreams.'

'Anything else?' Saffi had to run a little to keep up.

'Try not to go mad,' Figment offered, as if this was a choice.

He made no further comment. Saffi was simply grateful to take a shorter route. Even so, by the time they trudged around a cape and reached the next bay, she estimated they had been walking for at least half an hour. There was no way of knowing. When she checked her watch, she saw that it had stopped. Only when they arrived at a narrow inlet surmounted by cliffs did their guide speak again.

'Here we are.' He smiled his bland smile. 'Back door. You'll leave by another way, I expect. Can't go out the same way you came in.'

More fairy logic, Saffi thought to herself. The slopes of the island on this side were sheer: little of the house could be seen above the precipice, a turret or two at most. She preferred it that way. At the head of a beach piled with white stones was a triangular cave-mouth, yawning black as night. Figment led them towards it, toenails clicking on the stones.

'This is where I leave you,' he said. 'Forfeit House doesn't agree with me. Unless –' he eyed Saffi's bag – 'you'd spare more of those?'

Saffi knew there were only two rolls left, enough for herself and Birdy. She was about to decline, when she heard a strange sound. It began as a rasping and scraping, as if someone was running a metal spoon around a giant metal bowl. Soon, music welled up through the scraping, a single deep and sonorous note followed by harmonising ones. The effect was of many church bells tolling in unison. On and on they rang, so loud that Saffi stuck her fingers in her ears.

'What's happening?' she shouted to Figment over the cacophony.

He answered but she couldn't understand. Birdy also had his hands over his ears. Saffi gave up and waited for the noise to end, eyes screwed shut. After what seemed an age – it was probably a minute or two – the notes shifted to a lower register. She recognised the sound she had heard when they first arrived. This must be the tenth clock chime, slowed to the point where every harmonic was audible.

'The Bells of Heaven,' Figment said, when it was possible to speak again. 'They strike for twelve hours every twelfth day, when spheres align.'

He was standing rather too close, Saffi realised as she opened her eyes.

'That's not heaven,' she said. 'That's the clock in my grandparents' hall.'

Figment looked incredulous, as if she had claimed the earth was flat. 'Silly,' he scoffed. 'Why would a clock strike every twelve days?'

The last echoes of the chime were fading. Saffi opened her mouth to explain the time difference between their worlds, then decided she had other concerns.

'Thank you for helping us,' she told him. 'We appreciate it.'

'Remember.' Figment was all smiles and goodwill. 'Don't eat the food. Maybe I'll see you on the other side – or what's left of you.'

With that last piece of encouragement, he trotted away

across the sands. The mystery of his relationship to Treasure, if any, remained intact. Saffi took Birdy's hand and hurried into the dimly-lit cave, aware that they had only two chimes left. That appeared to translate into two hours in this world. Grandad said he had only ever spent an hour here. Somehow, they had to find Dad and Milo, and return to the mirror door before the last chime struck.

The cavern was large, larger than the one by Beacon Hill. At the back was a flight of stairs carved into solid rock.

Birdy hung back. 'You're sure you want to do this?' he asked.

'I have to try,' said Saffi. 'I couldn't live with myself otherwise.'

He seemed satisfied by that. Hand in hand, they began to climb the steps. The flight continued on through a tunnel. Once her eyes adjusted, Saffi was able to see her way well enough. A dusty yellowish gleam came from above.

At the top, the tunnel opened out to a square hall. It was empty, unfurnished except for hangings on the stone walls. Windows around the domed ceiling allowed in beams of late afternoon sun. But these filtered only partway through the air, picking up dust motes. In the shadows, she made out rich tapestries with courtly scenes. One showed a hunt in which a king pursued a white stag; another a queen in a garden, feeding the stag grapes. Archways stood where there were no hangings, two in the wall ahead and one beside them, to the right. There wasn't a sound in the place. Everything smelled of dust and disuse.

'Which way?' whispered Birdy.

There was something about the house – a silence, a loneliness – that made one want to whisper. Saffi considered the arches. The one immediately to the right led to a corridor with windows overlooking the beach. In the wall opposite, the right-hand passage carried on straight, while the left-hand one had stairs leading up.

'Why not up?' she said. 'We want to reach the main part of the house, don't we? That's on the other side of the ridge.'

He nodded. They moved across the hall. But as soon as they stepped through the left-hand archway, Saffi found that they were walking down the familiar stairs to the cave. The upside-down fairy logic had struck again.

'This place will drive me bonkers,' she said.

'I expect that's the idea,' remarked Birdy.

They plodded up to the hall again. This time, by mutual agreement, they turned around at the top and headed down – only to find themselves climbing up the left-hand stairs, as if this were a perfectly normal sequence of events. If steps could be smug, Saffi thought, these ones would be. The way they carried on after that, as any steps should, was insufferable. The flight ended at a gallery bathed in sunlight.

They must have been near the top of the house. When Saffi looked out of the windows, she saw a chaotic jumble of copper-clad rooftops, turrets and cupolas stained green. The view to the west was broken by a single tall structure that might house a hall. The corridor was so deathly still that her own breath sounded loud. Her footsteps made no noise on the green carpet as she and Birdy walked on.

'Can I ask you a question?' she whispered to him after a while.

By then, they were descending another flight of stairs at the end of the corridor. Luckily, these were straightforward.

'Go on,' he said.

'Have you ever been to this house before?'

They had arrived in another gallery with wood-panelled walls. Along each side were closed doors, between which hung a series of portraits. Some were covered in drapes to keep off dust. Both ends of the gallery had colourful stained glass windows, lit up by sunlight. One side showed a group of knights on horseback, while the other had a pack of hounds. The knights had green hair and the dogs red ears.

Saffi had asked the question because she didn't know the name of the boy beside her. And why were they holding hands?

'That's funny,' he answered. They had both stopped walking now. He looked as perplexed as she was. 'I can't remember. I'm Birdy, by the way. Have we met?'

'I'm Saffi,' she said. 'I can't remember you, either.'

It was strange. She was sure she had known only a short while ago what she was doing here, in this picture gallery, with this boy. The knowledge had evaporated like mist in the sun. That was a little worrying. But it was too quiet and dreamy in the house to worry much.

'Were we invited?' Birdy gazed around him.

'Let's hope it's by nobody in those paintings.' Saffi grimaced.

For the faces in the portraits on either side of the gallery – those without coverings – were without exception proud, cruel, or unpleasant in a way she couldn't define. The artist had taken care to show every hard glance, every mean curl of lip. The names of the people were written on brass plaques on the frames. They all belonged to one family. There was an Arabella, a Jack, a Margaret, several Henrys.

What an odd last name, Saffi mused. *True.*

'Why are we holding hands?' asked the boy. His name had slipped her mind again. Then: 'What's all this writing on mine?'

He held his palms out to show her. *Get Saffi's family. No food.* Glancing down, she found similar messages on her own. They were familiar, the words nagging at the corners of her mind. She realised suddenly that she had written them. *I'm Saffi,* she thought. She had a sense of an image coming into focus.

With that, her memories flooded back all at once. It must have been the same for Birdy because he looked horrified. The spell was broken.

'I forgot,' he gasped. 'Why I was here. You. Everything.'

Saffi felt dizzy with shock. It was horrible to realise how much she had forgotten between the upper gallery and this one. Any notion of what she was doing in the castle, every recollection of Dad and Milo, even her memories of Mum had disappeared. Only Forfeit House and the Lady remained. Somehow, she hadn't quite believed it was possible.

'They don't just take any memories,' she breathed. 'They take the ones you love.' She peered at the pictures. 'Look, these people are Trues. All my awful family. Those portraits are trophies. Like you'd hang up animal heads. We've got to put a stop to this, Birdy.'

He needed no further persuading. They held hands again – it had been a good idea, and a lucky escape – and hurried towards the stairwell at the end of the gallery. As they passed the last portrait, a drape fell away. The picture was of an old man with white hair and staring eyes, his face so haunted by regret that Saffi couldn't bear to look. She had already guessed the name on the brass plaque.

It was *Sir Henry True.*

19
Truth

After the episode in the picture gallery, the two of them pressed on. It had shaken Saffi to realise how easily she could forget. She didn't want to spend a minute longer in Forfeit House than she needed. Only one thing mattered: to find Dad and Milo, get them away.

By now, they had arrived in the more inhabited sections of the Lady's domain. The rooms were large and luxurious, with painted ceilings and crystal chandeliers. Images adorned the walls, familiar scenes of dancing maidens and shepherds but all, Saffi noticed, slightly odd, as if the artists weren't used to drawing people. Noses were too long, smiles too wide, ears pointed. Sometimes, a hoof or a tail peeked out from under a gown. This side of the house had been prepared for some gala event. Parquet floors were polished to a mirror shine, mantelpieces festooned with roses. Trestle tables were covered in crisp white linen. Beyond the veranda doors, stone terraces glowed pink in the setting sun.

It was all rather spectacular but Saffi had no time to admire it. Though the tide was still out, there was a gleam on the horizon that might have been water. If they were to reach the mirror door, she knew, it would have to be before waves covered the bay. Then, halfway across a magnificent, gilded ballroom, a sound – the first Saffi had heard in the house – stopped them in their tracks.

A peal of laughter echoed out, followed by the unmistakeable notes of a harp.

Saffi stood by Birdy, listening. It was difficult to work out where the music came from. The echoes were everywhere. When the piece was done, a faint sound of applause rang out. Voices cried *bravo* or *encore*.

'That way, I think,' said Birdy, pointing to a pair of double doors.

They passed through a lobby to what must be the entrance hall. It contained another imposing set of doors to the outside, as well as a great oak staircase. Try as they might, however, they couldn't locate the gathering. In the hall, the voices were coming from above. But as soon as they climbed the stairs, the noise grew faint. The upstairs corridors were quiet and still, flanked by wood-panelled doors; they opened one to find a bedroom equipped with a four-poster bed. They had no further luck downstairs. Beyond the front hall was another suite of galleries, culminating in a magnificent library and two-storey hexagonal chamber lined with books, silent as a tomb. The dome above it was made of glass. That was the only room Saffi was tempted to explore further.

At last, they returned to the entrance hall and staircase, roughly at the centre of the house where the voices were loudest. There was no sign of the company, who could be heard plainly at dinner, laughing and clinking glasses. Worse yet, Saffi could smell the food, a delicious odour of roast meat. She didn't forget the many warnings she had been given against eating the food in Forfeit House. Still, it was irksome to smell that while they wandered about, stymied – it was evident – by some spell. The Lady refused to be found.

'How about those sausage rolls,' Birdy said.

It seemed the best course for the present. They both sat down on the bottom step in the entrance hall. But when Saffi opened up the bag, then felt inside with growing consternation, the rolls were gone. The bag was empty, aside from Mum's letters and a few crumbs. She recalled Figment standing too close.

'He robbed me,' she said. 'Figment. There's nothing left. He must have stuck his ugly face in the bag while the chime rang. Gobbled them up.'

'Ah.' Birdy surveyed the doors in front of them. 'He did bring us to the right entrance. Call it payment.'

A sense of gloom settled on Saffi. Birdy looked just as hungry and tired as she felt. She wished that they could join the merry company upstairs. To sit with friends, and laugh, and eat delicious food . . .

'Why do I have this writing on—' she began, before remembering. 'Whoa!' she cried, jumping to her feet. 'We have to figure this place out, or we won't last five minutes.'

'Great.' He stood up to face her. 'I suppose that settles it.'

'Settles what?' asked Saffi.

He looked sad but determined. 'I'll stay here, in exchange for your family's freedom. I think the Lady might say yes.'

'No way.' Saffi folded her arms. 'I'll stay. You go, take Milo and Dad home.'

They glared at each other in silence, before a half-smile began to twitch at the corner of Birdy's mouth.

'What's so funny?' she asked.

He shook his head. 'We were trying so hard to get out of this. Now, we're arguing about who'll stay.'

He sat down again. She joined him. 'Why d'you think she'd say yes?'

'Well,' he answered slowly. 'The Lady didn't ask for owt, that time in cave. But she did say –' he frowned, trying to remember – 'she said, if I was ever tired of my life and wanted more, I was to come back.'

Saffi found herself thinking about the difference between Birdy's exchange and Sir Henry's. Sir Henry had greedily waylaid the Lady, insisted on his wishes. Birdy just wanted to help his mum. This, if her own mum's point held true, changed the deal. Maybe the price wasn't so heavy for him.

'You know how it is when you're small,' he was saying. 'You don't understand. She meant, I could live with her if I wanted.'

Saffi waited until she could catch his eye. 'I'm not going to let you stay,' she said. 'We're going to get out of this. All of us, together.'

They both fell silent. The murmur of voices rose from

behind, where the invisible meal in the invisible dining room went on.

'We've tried everything,' Saffi sighed after a moment. 'Going in the opposite direction. Moving. Waiting. Why can't we find them?'

'Maybe we just can't.' Birdy turned to her with one of his rare, bright smiles. 'I don't care. I'm glad we met, Saf. I'd rather fail a thousand times with you than win with the Lady. That's the truth – hand on heart.'

He placed his hand on his chest, as he had with Piccola. Saffi grinned back, both pleased and embarrassed by the compliment.

'I'm glad, too. It's the only Gift I'd ever ask for. A friend.'

Then, another thought occurred. 'What if –' she turned to Birdy in excitement – 'we didn't ask at all? What if, like Mum said, we tried—'

She meant to say, *a different spirit*. But even as she spoke, a familiar rasping noise started up. The eleventh chime had begun, its drawn-out scrape followed by a bass note and harmonics as before. The music was so loud on this side of the house that the windows shook. Saffi could only crouch on the step with her fingers in her ears, her head bowed against Birdy's shoulder. They leaned against each other for a long while, eyes closed, until the sound reached the lower end of its register and became more bearable. Saffi opened her eyes and unplugged her ears – only to find herself staring at a row of people.

A group of pages dressed in green livery stood at the foot

of the stairs. They held platters of cheese, fruit and cake, waiting for her and Birdy to allow them by.

'You are welcome in my house,' said a familiar voice. 'But I'm afraid you'll have to move aside. My servants must pass.'

And there she was, when they scrambled up and turned around: the Fairy Queen, Lady of Forfeit House, more resplendent than ever in a green gown embroidered with thread of gold. A gold circlet adorned her temples. She stood at the top of the steps, in front of a set of double doors that simply hadn't been there before. Beyond them was the great hall Saffi had glimpsed from the upstairs gallery.

'Won't you join me for dinner?' said the Lady.

She glanced from Saffi to Birdy in amusement, as if she had known where they were all along. Then, she walked back to the hall, where a glittering company sat at a feast.

The Lady's banqueting table was draped in damask cloth, with room for about twenty people on each side. The remains of an elaborate meal were spread out. Platters piled high with quail or pheasant sat alongside bowls of fruit and salad, cold cuts and jellies, white bread and brown. A roast suckling pig lay on a silver platter at the centre. Only the head remained, apple in mouth. Decanters of chased silver stood at the guests' elbows; they drank from goblets of cut crystal. Hanging over all was a chandelier made of deer antlers. The windows above allowed in the last rays of evening sun.

To her left, at one end of the table, Saffi recognised the Lord, black and brooding in his horned headdress. The other revellers resembled those at the B&B, strange and ostentatious, even repellent in their glamour. Feathers, silks and jewels abounded, though no one was as magnificent as the Lady. She moved across the hall to take her place opposite the Lord, where a page drew out a chair. The conversation died away as the whole company turned to stare at Saffi and Birdy.

Then Saffi gave a gasp, before clapping her hand over her mouth. For in the midst of the gathering were Dad and Milo, their rumpled, ordinary selves in sharp contrast to the rest of the guests. Milo was wearing his green *Milosaurus* T-shirt, Dad his usual tan sweater. Their expressions as they looked at her were just like everyone else's, politely curious. There was no spark of recognition.

'Remember,' Birdy whispered. 'Whatever happens—'

He couldn't finish, as the Lady spoke again. 'Friends,' she announced, 'I am pleased to be able to introduce two more guests to our company, though the hour is late. We welcome Persephone, daughter of William True, to our home.'

She turned to Birdy. 'Our little bird needs no introduction. Greetings, Jack Lythe. You have done well.' She beckoned him to her side. 'You shall serve me tonight.'

Done well? wondered Saffi with a twinge of misgiving. She watched in confusion as Birdy hesitated, then went to stand by the Lady's chair, just as if he were one of the pages. These last had come in to set down their platters. Some stood behind the guests to wait on them, while others carried out dishes from the main course. It was strange to see Birdy do the same, bending forward with his silver flagon as the Lady held up her goblet. Was he playing for time?

'Oh yes.' The Lady smiled: Saffi's bewilderment hadn't escaped her. 'Years ago, I gave him a Gift. Now, he gives me one. I don't suppose he told you.'

Birdy's gaze darted towards Saffi, anxious. She remembered what he said on the stairs, that he would rather fail with her than win with the Lady. Their host was trying to drive a wedge between them. She wouldn't succeed. In any case, the Lord was speaking to her now, gesturing to an empty chair on his right.

'Will you not join us, Persephone True, like the rest of your family?' He gave a disdainful smile. 'I trust you enjoyed our picture gallery.'

Saffi was in a quandary. She knew that her refusal to sit down in the face of his request would seem rude. And these people prized courtesy above all else. She also knew that if she took her place in that company, or ate even a bite of that food, she would lose all recollection of who she was. She gathered up her courage.

'My Lord and Lady,' she began, as formal as she knew how, her heart beating fast. 'Thank you. I'm honoured by your invitation.'

She paused, racking her brains for an excuse that would neither offend, nor oblige her to join them. 'I came to beg for mercy,' she went on. 'Please. Release my father and brother. Let us go.'

She appealed to the Lady as she had once appealed to

Piccola. But after a moment of staring at her in unfeigned surprise, her host tilted back her head and laughed. The whole gathering laughed with her, as it had in the guest suite, a chorus of hoots, giggles, barks and cackles. Saffi winced, waiting for the noise to die down.

'Ah me,' said the Lady at last. 'You do amuse. You ask to be released from your bond. But what, in the name of all that is Seen or Unseen, would convince me to do that? Your father and brother made their choice.' She gave a little flick of her fingers in the direction of Dad and Milo. 'In return, they have a Gift. Should I not honour our agreement?'

As Saffi looked on in amazement, her face began to change. The Lady's features altered, until the fairy with her halo of golden hair was gone, and in her place was the exact likeness of Mum. But this was Mum from long ago, before the headscarves and IV drips: Mum with dimples in her cheeks and fizzy dark curls. Milo and Dad gazed at her, adoring. This is what Milo wanted so badly, Saffi thought. This was why he was willing to go anywhere, agree to anything. Her own eyes were wet as she witnessed that memory. Longing twisted inside her.

But it was only that. A memory. Not true, not real. She preferred the letter, real ink on a page. She touched the envelope through the bag at her side.

'I gave them what they wanted,' the Lady was saying with Mum's mouth. 'I could give you the same. You are your father's helper, your brother's carer. Let me lift that burden. Be at peace here, with your family, in my house.'

212

Saffi averted her eyes from the Mum-that-wasn't-Mum. This was the second time the Lady had offered her peace. *Stay uncomfortable,* she remembered.

'I'd rather have the truth,' she said. Her voice had gone hoarse.

'Accept, and it will feel the same.'

'It's not,' Saffi answered with sudden intensity. 'It's a lie. Even if I don't know it.'

She had expected that to anger her host. Instead, when she looked back, the Lady was watching her with quiet attention. The resemblance to Mum had faded.

'A worthy answer,' she said. 'Yet it doesn't solve our problem. You beg for mercy on behalf of those you love. But they accepted my offer. The fact is, Trues have always accepted it. How can you ask for mercy for your loved ones, when your ancestors showed no mercy to anyone else?'

'That's not fair!' protested Saffi.

'Fair.' The Lord almost spat out the word. He hadn't spoken in a while, and now his tone chilled her. 'When is life *fair*? There are always some poor souls to hand, willing to trade their freedom for a pittance. Oh, had you asked your forebears, they would have told you it was all perfectly legal. A contract, signed and sealed. Be that as it may, they bought and sold misery. To them, life was cheap.'

His gaze was on the pages. Saffi realised these last were different to the rest of the company, less exquisite and otherworldly. Their faces, aloof and fairy-like now, might once have been human. They looked like someone's storybook idea of royal pages, dressed in costumes no one would normally wear: exotic silks and brocades, jewelled turbans, green slippers with turned-up toes. Like statues in a cabinet, she thought with a shiver.

She had a horrible feeling she ought to know who they were.

The Lord's smile was cynical. 'Observe the True legacy,' he said, pointing to each child in turn. 'Calcutta. Bombay. Madras, as people used to call those places. Though by all accounts, some boys were recruited closer to home, in your English slums. All taken, all sold, never to be seen again. That voyage on the *White Hind* was the last journey they'd ever make. Was that *fair*?'

Saffi understood. These were the young people Sir Henry had duped. They looked no older than she was. It was awful to imagine those boys shipped off to who knew where, to die or disappear. She wondered if they were somehow still alive, if she might save them.

'They are shadows of the past,' the Lord said, as if he guessed her hope. 'That was Sir Henry's game, and it is played. There is no one left to save.'

Saffi had to ask herself why, if the Lord and Lady hated Henry True so much, they had agreed to his appalling deal in the first place. Were they as bound by the magic as her family? Whatever the truth, they considered it her responsibility now. There was no more to say. The Lady was silent and withdrawn, gazing down at her lap.

'So much youth and life, squandered for a bit of gold.'

The Lord's voice deepened on the last word. 'How does that make you feel?'

'Terrible,' said Saffi.

It didn't help her to feel terrible, though. She was beginning to doubt there was a way out of this deal at all. Then, she recalled Birdy's question. *How do we talk to them?*

If the Lord and Lady wanted a game, maybe she should give them one.

'Which is why,' she added, trying to muster up a confidence she didn't feel, 'it needs to end. No more Gifts. I propose a test. Winner takes all.'

It was worth a try. The Lord, at least, referred to the True deal as if it were a contest of sorts, though lives were at stake. It was the only idea she could come up with anyway. Her hosts were silent. The revellers at the table looked on as she waited, heart thumping, afraid that she had offended them again. But when the Lady answered, her tone was calm.

'What kind of test?'

'A game. You choose which.' Saffi couldn't have decided on one. 'If I succeed, I take my father, brother and Birdy home. This contract ends.'

A rumble of outrage rose from around the table. But the Lady only raised her hand for silence.

'And if you lose?' she said.

'Then I accept your invitation.' Saffi swallowed dryness in her throat. 'You can do what you like with us.'

'Your terms,' said the Lady, 'are acceptable. The challenge I propose is a simple one. I will ask you three questions.

If you answer rightly, you may leave my house along with those you mention. If you fail, you all stay here as my guests. Do we agree?'

Saffi saw Birdy watching her from behind the Lady's high-backed chair.

'We agree,' she replied.

'Then,' said the Lady with a brilliant smile, 'let us begin.'

❧ 20 ❧
Courage

The Lady rose from her place and began to pace the length of the table. She was clearly enjoying herself.

'My first question is this,' she said. '*Small am I, great am I. Always seen, never known. A friend far from home. What am I?*'

Saffi grasped in dismay that by 'questions', her host meant riddles. Of course. There was nothing more fairy-like. She tried to empty her mind and concentrate on the puzzle, but couldn't think of an answer. What was both great and small, seen but not known, and a friend? Her gaze wandered over the gathering, lingering on Dad and Milo's impassive faces. It came to rest on Birdy, standing still and silent by the Lady's chair.

What have I done, she thought in panic. I can't win.

The sunlight had dropped beneath the level of the windows, plunging the hall in shadows. The candles in their bizarre chandelier glittered bright. Saffi was beginning to wonder if she would fail before she had answered the first question, when she found herself remembering how she used to beg Mum to tell her the tale of 'the faraway light'. Mum would say: *This is a story from long ago, when our ancestors spoke a language called Sanskrit. Everything had just been invented, even night and day. The first light came from a fire, far, far away across the universe. It was so far that by the time that light arrived here, the fire might be out. You'd never know. That's why you can't really know—*

'A star,' she said.

The company stirred, whispering. But the Lady smiled. 'Know thyself, Tara True.'

She tapped two fingers at her throat. Saffi realised she had reached up to touch the pendant again, and dropped her hand, embarrassed. But the Lady had already moved on to the next question.

'That one was easy,' she said. 'The next won't be. The answer is stronger than magic:

'This garden may be friend or foe.
Plant only sweet fruit. Walls are no good here.
Be generous and invite the neighbours in,
But watch out for snakes.'

Then she faced Saffi with a charming smile, as if to say, *Aren't we having fun.*

How could Saffi answer that? What was a garden, a friend and an enemy as well? She doubted it was a literal place, but couldn't think what it might be or why it was stronger than magic. It didn't help that she felt faint with hunger. Her stomach kept growling when she caught a whiff of the food on the table. Her thoughts seemed to spill out of her head.

'Do you forfeit?' asked the Lady after a long silence. Her green eyes shone too bright in the darkened hall, as if they had a phosphorescent quality.

'Just a moment longer,' pleaded Saffi.

'Be quick,' said the Lady. 'I have slowed time, not stopped it. I fear I will be old and grey before you answer.'

She began pacing again. The other guests at the table were whispering to each other, glancing sidelong at Saffi. They expected her to fail. She expected herself to fail. The Lady was too clever. She could see the gleam of the Lord's eyes behind his mask, waiting for her to admit defeat. Birdy, for his part, didn't look at her at all. He was doing something, she noticed. He had his hand on his chest, rubbing as if to loosen a feeling of tightness. *Hand on heart*, she remembered suddenly.

'Your moment is up.' The Lady's smile vanished when she saw Saffi looking at Birdy. 'Do you forfeit?'

'A heart,' Saffi said at once. 'The answer is a heart.'

There were murmurs of objection from the guests. The Lady gave Birdy a searching look. He dropped his eyes again, a model of obedience.

'Very well,' she answered, slow. 'In that case, we come to the last question. You say you wish to bring your family home. But I put it to you that you don't know who they are. Not really. What makes your father and brother so different from anyone else, worthy of my mercy? Can you find them for me now? Show me where they are, and I will let them go.'

Saffi was relieved. This question would be easy. She had already seen Dad and Milo, remembered where they sat. She opened her mouth to answer, even took a step forward as she searched the company for the green T-shirt, the rumpled tan sweater.

Then, the realisation struck. She couldn't see those familiar forms. The revellers were dressed in ostentatious finery. Worse yet, she couldn't recognise any of the faces. A sea of mask-like countenances stared at her. She wondered if Dad and Milo were here at all.

'I assure you, they are,' said the Lady, as if she had read her mind.

For the first time since their arrival in the house, Saffi felt the cold brush of despair. Birdy, too, was frozen in place by the table. He had no answer for her.

'Do you forfeit?' asked the Lady.

The smile had returned to her lips but it was a cruel one. This was a trick, Saffi was sure. The Lady was cheating. But so, she remembered, had she.

'Will you let me take a closer look?' she asked in a bid for time.

The Lady gave a pretty shrug, sitting down in her chair. 'Go as close as you like. Walk about the table. But do not dawdle, and do not talk to the guests. They won't help you.'

She sipped from her goblet, to all appearances bored. Saffi began to make a tour of the banqueting table, as slow as she dared. A hum of conversation rose again in the hall as the guests continued their meal. Knives and spoons clinked on plates, while the pages bent down with silent solicitude to serve cake, fruits, ices. As Saffi passed by each chair, she searched the face of the person sitting in it, hoping to see a trace of her father or brother. But there was none. The guests in the hall all looked perfect. There were no shadows under their eyes, no laugh lines at their mouths. They had the same smooth expression. Saffi hated it. Grandma was more beautiful with her wrinkles. Even Lily had more appeal.

'Well?' asked the Lady, before she was halfway around. 'Choose, or I will.'

'Almost there, my Lady.' Saffi tried to be as polite as she could be.

'I don't know why I'm such a soft touch.' The Lady sighed to herself.

It was difficult to stay focussed. Saffi wanted to shout to Dad and Milo, beg them to identify themselves. But she guessed they wouldn't be able to. She walked by the Lord, who sat still as a hulking statue, then up the far side of the table. Still the revellers talked and laughed, never looking at her. There was no choosing between their perfect, fatuous faces. Saffi could have wept. At last, she approached the end of her circuit and the Lady's place, where Birdy stood with his silver tray and flagon.

That gave her an idea. Just as she passed him by, she reached out with a quick movement and knocked the flagon off the tray.

With a clatter and bang, it fell to the floor, splashing crimson liquid. The company fell silent. Everyone stared as Birdy dived under the table to retrieve it. In that instant of distraction, Saffi kept her eyes on the guests. She noticed that two were more startled by the interruption. One had dropped his spoon while the other miscalculated a bite, smearing chocolate on his chin. The clumsy imperfections seemed beautiful to Saffi.

'Those two!' she cried, singling them out before the Lady could speak.

Immediately, the recognisable forms of Dad and Milo reappeared. Dad was the one who dropped the spoon, while Milo's chin was a mess. They gazed about them as if they had just woken from a dream. Saffi could have cheered. But the Lady had also changed. She looked taller, menacing as she rose from her high-backed chair. Her eyes shone green as glacier water. A babble of protest went up from the crowd.

'You cheated,' said the Lady.

Her voice sent a shudder through Saffi. Dad stood up, staring at his hosts in astonishment. Milo ran into his arms. Saffi edged around the table to where Birdy climbed out. A cacophony of voices, gibbering or howling with rage, filled the hall. The gathering swayed to its collective feet, crying *cheat, cheat*. Saffi reached her hand out to Birdy.

'Oh no you don't,' said the Lady.

Even as Saffi grasped his right hand, she stepped swiftly up to take his left, so that they stood on each side of him. The Lady laughed then, but the sound was cold.

'So that's how it is,' she said. She turned to Birdy. 'Why do you seek to leave, little bird? I gave you all you desired. Comfort. Happiness. And this.'

She reached into a pocket of her gown, withdrawing something. 'Don't you want it?' she asked, holding out the carved flute.

Saffi could see Birdy gazing at it with longing. But the Lady held on to his other hand, which meant that he would have to let go of Saffi's to take it.

'I'll find another,' he said.

'As you wish.' The Lady put the flute away.

'Please. You said he could go.' Saffi summoned up every ounce of courage that remained to her, faced with those icy eyes.

'You cheated,' the Lady said. 'You may take your family, but he stays.'

'Go, Saffi,' Birdy urged her. 'While you still can.'

Saffi glanced over her shoulder. As they were talking, an extraordinary transformation had overtaken the company in the hall. The guests were coming undone, their elegant bodies and faces bulging, distorting, splitting at the sides. Feathers and illusions dropped away as they resumed what must be their true forms: dozens of sprites, piled on top of each other like acrobats at a circus. The vaguely bipedal figures they had constructed disintegrated as they jumped off and scattered through the room, hooting with glee. Another change, no less drastic, came over the food on the table. The fine cakes and fruit were gone, replaced by piles of ashes and leaves. Saffi's mouth felt dry as she imagined eating them. As to the pages, those 'shadows of the past', they had vanished altogether.

The Lord during this time had reared up to twice his former height. His human form fell away, as if that was the costume. He was a massive black stag that tossed up its antlers and stamped its hoofs, bellowing with rage. Dad backed slowly away with Milo in his arms, making for the door. He signed for Saffi to follow. But she didn't let go of Birdy's hand.

'I won't leave without him,' she told the Lady.

The stag uttered another deafening bellow and charged at the sprites, who screeched and dashed for the doors. Dad stepped back with Milo as a torrent of them ran past, wailing. A moment later, the stag thundered out with a whirl of black hoofs. Its antlers barely cleared the lintel. Saffi heard it skid and crash down the stairs, then another dim crash from below. The Lady waited for the noise to die down.

'Good,' she said when silence returned. 'We shall see what you are made of.'

All at once, it wasn't Birdy's hand that Saffi held, but the wing of a great white swan. She almost let go as the creature thrashed in her grip. But she collected her wits and held on, ducking to avoid the huge orange beak that stabbed this way and that. Somehow, she knew that she had to maintain her nerve. This was a test of mettle. The Lady stood back.

'Is that not enough?' she asked, as Saffi hung grimly on. She gave a flick of her wrist. 'How about this?'

Now, to Saffi's horror, a white serpent writhed in her grasp as she held it by the neck. The snake spread its hood in warning and flicked its forked tongue. Her instinct was to hurl it as far away as possible. Instead, she held on, keeping it at arm's length. She could hear her dad shouting at her to *let go*.

'Still not enough?' The Lady raised both of her arms. 'Very well.'

Then Saffi's heart almost stopped, for it was a white lion she held. The animal was a young one, nowhere near fully grown but heavier than she was, all rippling muscles and shaggy fur. It twisted in her arms, staring at her out of bright blue eyes. Then it roared, baring yellow fangs in a pink mouth. Saffi fought the electric instinct to *run*. Instead, she kept one arm locked around the lion and with the other hand grabbed the loose fur at its neck. She waited for what seemed an eternity, eyes shut tight for the next change.

It never came. After a while, the lion's struggles lessened, as if it understood that she meant it no harm. It could have ripped her face with one swipe of its razor claws, or clamped those teeth down on her arm. Instead, it slowly settled. When Saffi opened her eyes, there was only Birdy, wincing as she clutched a handful of his hair.

'Maybe let go now,' he muttered.

As she released him, she heard the Lady's cry of rage. They had been kneeling on the floor. When they rose, Saffi found their host towering over them with eyes like green fire.

'Traitor,' she hissed to Birdy. 'I'll tear you limb from limb!'

That was when Saffi knew that the wager was over, and the Lady had lost. Neither she nor Birdy waited to see what she would do, dashing away to join Dad and Milo by the door. They ran pell-mell downstairs, bursting out through the main doors of the house onto a wide stone balcony. The sky above it was a luminous mother-of-pearl colour.

Despite the Lady's threat, Saffi stopped at the balustrade to look out. Dad halted with her. From here, a series of ramps led down to the postern gate and beach they had seen on their arrival. Birdy was already hurrying towards them, followed by Milo. But it was the sight beyond the beach that gave Saffi pause. The sun was a fiery red ball balanced on the horizon. Beneath it, stretching out in all directions, was the sea. Bright waters lapped against the shore. The brown sand was gone.

'Is this—?' began Dad in wonder.

'The other world,' said Saffi. 'Yes.'

'What are you waiting for?' Birdy called up from below. 'She's coming!'

The urgency in his voice made Saffi glance back. There was the Lady, striding out of the house with a look that sent them all scrambling for the ramps.

'Do you think you can simply return to your old lives, unchanged?' she called after them. 'Think again!'

Saffi tried not to think what would happen if the Lady caught up. She hurried with the others down to the postern gate and beach, to crunch over piled shells to the water. Birdy waded straight in. The water was barely up to his ankles. Saffi splashed in after him with a dizzying sense of walking into the sky. Huge ripples spread at her feet. Dad was still trying to understand what had happened as he followed with Milo.

'Where are we headed?' He gazed at the empty horizon in puzzlement.

'Back through the mirror door,' said Saffi. 'It works with the clock.'

'So Anoush was right.' Then, he looked appalled. 'Good lord, what have I been doing?' He gripped Saffi's arm. 'I forgot everything!'

'Magic,' she said, pulling him along. 'I'll tell you later. We have to hurry.'

She was painfully aware that they had to find the door before the final stroke of midnight, though she saw no mirror frame ahead. It might have been an hour since the last chime. Milo kept glancing back as they splashed on.

'She's on the stairs,' he reported. 'She doesn't look happy.' Then, he peered to their left. 'There's something else, too. A dog? Is that thing dangerous?'

Figment, thought Saffi. She could see him now. He slunk alongside them, keeping his distance. She shook her head at Milo but said no more, for just then another, all-too-familiar sound echoed out. Dim at first, then louder, the scrape of bell-notes began. The twelfth chime had struck.

'The door,' she gasped, breaking into a run. 'Find the door!'

They all ran on together, stumbling through the shallows.

But they were running blind. Even after the rocks where they met Figment, Saffi saw nothing that resembled a mirror. To her alarm, the Lady was gaining on them, too, striding through the waters as the bell chime rang. She seemed gigantic. All her finery was gone; she was draped in purple ribbons of seaweed. And still there was no door in sight, no mirror frame.

Then, Saffi saw it – the evening star, glinting in the sky to her right. *So you'll always come home.* She changed course to head towards it, waving to the others. But they had another problem. Ever since the chime began, Saffi had noticed a white line on the horizon. It was an approaching wave, she grasped now, low but very long, stretching across the bay. There was no avoiding it. Even as she cried out a warning to Dad and Birdy, the foam rushed up to her legs. The water that followed was deeper, turbulent, swirling around her calves. And that wasn't all. Another, higher line was visible, rolling swiftly over the first.

The next wave hit hard and fast. It came up past Saffi's knees and she lost a boot to it. She had to kick off the other and walk in her socks, praying that they would find the door before the waters swept them away. Dad carried Milo in his arms.

'True child!'

She heard the Lady's voice calling from behind, loud enough to pierce the chime-din. Looking back, she saw that her enemy had closed the distance between them, her eyes shining like stars. She was a real giant now, big as a tree, her skin and hair grey as stone. Saffi didn't answer, struggling on. But the water dragged at her and she fell behind. She was glancing back when the third wave hit. This one reached up to her thighs, so strong that it nearly knocked her over.

'True child!' came the Lady's voice once more.

It took Saffi a moment to regain her balance. The others waded on. She heard their glad cries ahead. Then, she saw what they saw. A rod, or slot of light – it was the oddest-looking thing, perhaps the height of a man – hung over the sea. Dad was holding Milo up to it, pushing him in. He vanished. After that, he helped Birdy up. In between the two, a quadruped shape leaped into the light. So Figment must have crossed, too. The waters were up to Saffi's waist. She had to push against them with all her might. Her father shouted something she couldn't hear, holding his hand out. She had almost reached the light.

'True child,' said the Lady for a third time.

The sound was so deep and booming that Saffi had to turn around. The Fairy Queen loomed up, huge as a hill. She could have plucked Saffi out of the water like a toy. But she didn't. There was no trace of anger in her face. Her eyes were liquid silver. If anything, she looked sad. She had scooped something up in her hand, which she let trickle through her fingers. Saffi realised it was shells from the beach.

'The dreams of men are hollow things.' Her voice was cavernous. 'They fill this world with husks.'

The chime music had shifted to a lower register, much to

Saffi's relief. But that also told her the door was closing. She had only a few seconds left.

'They used to dream wonders for me.' The Queen sighed. 'Living arias. Cathedrals of faith. What do they give me now? Paltry dreams of wealth and power.'

She flicked the shells away. 'I am alone. Will you not stay, Tara Persephone? I welcome the company of truth and courage.'

Saffi could hear her father calling, begging her to hurry up and grab his hand. Why she did what she did next, she couldn't tell. Maybe it was because something in the giant's face still reminded her of Mum.

'I can't,' she said. 'But why not visit us? You'd be welcome.'

As she said it, there was a sharp crack like thunder from above, accompanied by a flash of light. At the same time, she felt Dad's grip close around her wrist. Then she was pulled into the light, stretched by it like a piece of chewing gum. An instant later, she was tumbling out onto the hall floor at Fortune House, kneeling beside her father in a torrent of seawater. The last echoes of the chimes faded. Dark shapes milled about her; voices rose up in an angry hubbub.

Saffi paid them no heed, gazing at the mirror. For the glass had cracked from side to side. A diagonal split ran from the swan on the left to the lion on the right.

There was no more sea.

21
And Last

Someone was insisting that it must be a burst water main. That person had seen this sort of thing before, at her aunt's place in Harrogate. The old joints rusted through under the floor where you couldn't get to them, and one fine day they fell apart. The person said that she could get Dad the number of an excellent plumber who often worked for them at the York office. She could ask for it tomorrow . . .

'You all right?' whispered Dad, helping Saffi up.

Saffi understood that she had been in a state of shock, or half-asleep for the past minute or two, sitting in a puddle with her clothes sopping wet. She stood up slowly to gain her bearings. The hall was splattered with seawater. Lily was talking about plumbers to Dad. For the briefest moment, Saffi wondered whether she had imagined everything up to that point, like a fever dream. Then she glimpsed Treasure, or rather Figment under one of the hall chairs, back in poodle form. He winked at her out of one mad fairy eye.

Grandad, Mr Lythe and Birdy were standing in a knot by the front door, accompanied by two police officers in yellow hi-vis jackets. Grandma had hobbled over to give Milo one of her talcum-scented hugs. He looked sheepish but pleased as she crushed him against her.

'You had us going there, lad,' she murmured. 'You're daft as a brush. Know that?'

'I'm sorry, Grandma,' he said. Then he glanced at Saffi, mournful. 'So sorry.'

'It's all right,' answered Saffi.

But her attention was on the group by the door. Something was wrong. Mr Lythe was raising his voice, dissatisfied with an explanation he had been given.

'I don't care,' he said. 'When I asked where my son was, that man didn't have decency to tell me. No, no,' he interrupted, when one of the police officers began to say they should all go home and get some rest. 'You've seen my boy's not to blame. Now, that man should explain issen.'

He crossed his arms over his chest, bristling at Grandad, who bristled right back. Birdy stood wet and bedraggled, caught between the two of them.

'Can't keep track of his own, Detective Inspector,' Grandad remarked to the woman officer. 'So he blames me.'

Saffi was tired. It was past midnight after a very long day. But it still irritated her that these two men could almost lose everything they held dear – she was sure Grandad guessed where they had been, more or less – and still be more interested in bickering with each other. She marched over to them, splashing through puddles in her wet socks.

'Don't know what Birdy's told you, but here's how it

went,' she said as they stared in surprise. 'Milo walked down to the sea caves on his own. Right, Milo?' She turned to her brother, who nodded, before going on. 'Birdy saw him and followed, because he knew the danger. He saved Milo's life. So you can stop arguing now.'

It was as much of the truth as was possible to say. 'What she's not told you is she had a huge part in all that,' Birdy put in. 'I'd be lost without her.'

Lily's chattering voice, Saffi noticed, had faded away. She and Dad had gone off to the kitchen. The inspector looked annoyed.

'Why d'you not say so before?' she asked. 'We've had a team out for hours.'

'Because,' Saffi said, 'our families don't listen to us. When Birdy and I say we're friends, they get upset like it's illegal. We're sorry you were called out for nothing. But we can't help it if they believe the worst of each other.'

'Aye,' Birdy muttered with feeling.

The inspector raised her eyebrow at Grandad and Mr Lythe. 'Is this true?'

Both men were embarrassed. 'Didn't realise he'd done that,' Grandad began with a swift glance at Birdy. 'That he'd gone after my grandson.'

'Wouldn't change owt if you had,' said Mr Lythe.

They were ready to go at it again, Saffi realised. Nothing was able to end this feud, not even fairy magic. But the inspector intervened.

'Sounds to me like this has been cleared up.' She turned

to Birdy. 'Well done, son. Glad you were about to stop something we'd all –' here she gave Grandad and Mr Lythe a pointed look – 'regret. Now, if you don't mind – it's late.'

And that was that, to Saffi's delight. The officers didn't question her story now that Milo was home safe. Instead, they bid everyone goodnight and went back to their car, relieved to be done with the issue. By then, Mr Lythe was also steering Birdy out of the door, a protective hand on his shoulder.

'Come on, son,' he said. 'Some folk don't know a good turn if it hits 'em in face.'

'Just a minute, Thomas, if you please,' Grandma called to him.

Mr Lythe stopped as if someone had pulled his strings. Grandma waved to the police officers as they drove away, before turning to the two men, each of whom refused to meet the other's eye.

'Shake on it,' she said. Her tone was firm. 'Right now. Both of you. Go on,' she told her husband when he hesitated. 'No more prideful nonsense. And,' she went on as an afterthought, 'you're not letting Tom's park fail after this. You're giving him a loan, fair terms. Till he gets back on his feet. Understood?'

Grandad glowered but didn't contradict her. Instead, he stuck his hand out like a plank of wood at Mr Lythe. It was like seeing two boys in school, forced by a teacher to end a fist fight. Mr Lythe accepted Grandad's hand with a wary look but addressed himself to Grandma.

'Because it's you, Marge,' he grumbled. 'But we don't need charity.'

'Not another word,' Grandma said shortly as Grandad opened his mouth. 'Think of this as making amends.'

She was talking about the True legacy, Saffi grasped. Grandad seemed to know it, for he held his tongue. Birdy's father, meanwhile, had his arm around his son as they walked back to the rusty pickup. Saffi stared after them in bemusement. Where was furious Mr Lythe?

'See you soon,' Birdy whispered as they passed her.

There was a buoyancy in his step, climbing into the pickup, that she had never seen before. He was happy, though whether that was because he had escaped the power of the Fairy Queen or because his dad was proud of him, Saffi couldn't guess. He even held himself straighter.

'How about a cup of yummy hot cocoa, everyone?' asked Grandma as they watched the truck's taillights disappear.

Yummy, thought Saffi about a quarter of an hour later, seated at the kitchen table with Dad, Milo and her grandparents, wasn't the word she would have chosen for the scalding, milky concoction in her cup, already forming a skin on top. But it had been made with love at half past midnight by Grandma, still hobbling about on crutches. Lily was gone. She appeared to have left by the back door along with Treasure, without waiting to say goodbye. The rest of them came into the kitchen to find Dad alone at the table, staring down at his hands. He hadn't said much since, though he lifted a sleepy Milo onto his knee and let him drowse there.

Seeing the two of them like that reminded Saffi of how long it had been since Dad held Milo. He had done that – carried his son, comforted him – more in the past hour than he had in the year since Mum died. He accepted Mum's letter when Saffi offered it, reading it while she gave a full account of the events at Forfeit House. His expression was thoughtful.

'And you're sure the deal's off?' Grandad asked Saffi. 'No more Gifts?'

He had listened to her description of the riddles, as well as the final contest with the Lady, with close attention. Saffi made sure to spell out the risk Birdy had taken in helping them, his willingness to stay behind to buy their freedom.

'Must be,' she said. 'You saw the mirror.'

'You know,' Dad broke his silence then, gazing down at Mum's notes, 'I wonder if it wasn't your invitation that finally did it. Instead of taking, you gave. Just like Mum says. You approached the Lady in a different spirit.'

It was what Saffi had realised on the stairs in Forfeit House. 'Does it always work like that?' she turned to Grandad. 'To end a fairy deal, you turn it inside out?'

'I didn't know there was a way to end it.' Her grandfather darted Dad an apologetic look. 'I wouldn't talk to Anoush. On my high horse about keeping family secrets. If I had, we might have avoided this.'

'You wouldn't talk,' said Dad. 'But I wouldn't listen.

I don't know why. I thought . . .' he rubbed his hands through his hair. 'I thought she was so sick, she couldn't be right.'

Then he looked at Saffi. 'I owe you a sincere apology.'

Saffi couldn't find any words. But she got up and went to give him a kiss. His cheek, unshaved, pricked her lips. It felt like happiness.

'Right pair of fools we are,' sighed Grandad.

Grandma caught Saffi's eye with a look that meant: *He said it, we didn't.* But she squeezed her husband's hand.

'Chin up, Henry,' she said. 'We've all of us been too proud.' Then she glanced at Dad. 'Speaking of which, where's that Lily?'

'Ah.' Dad cleared his throat. 'I said I'd reconsidered the whole house sale idea. She got offended, I think. Said we weren't worth her time.'

'She's a mardy one.' Grandma sipped on her cocoa. 'Pay it no mind.'

Milo, Saffi noticed, had fallen asleep in their father's lap, his breathing regular. She felt waves of fatigue herself. But a husky little voice roused her.

'That may partly be our fault,' said Piccola.

The lady sprite was standing on the shelf above the table, between her grinning husband and a tattered copy of *Joy of Cooking*. They had been listening in sprite stealth mode. Dad was taken aback but gave a nod of greeting.

'I'm sorry, Mr True,' Piccola went on, bobbing him a curtsey. 'We may have given your lady friend the teeniest, tiniest truth draught. In her tea.' She darted Saffi a guilty glance. 'Perhaps it showed up a side of her you didn't like.'

'That's just it,' Dad said. 'Wouldn't surprise me if she'd been frightened or angry. But she didn't notice a thing. Not even when I fell out of a mirror.'

'Was she connected to the Lady?' Saffi asked Piccola. 'It's just that the creature who helped us in the other world – Figment – I think he's her dog.'

'Not one of our people,' said Piccola with a sniff of disdain. 'There's all sorts of riffraff who cross between worlds. No loyalty to anyone.'

'Lily was my punishment.' Dad spoke slowly, as if grasping the full extent of what he had done. 'I knew better. But I turned my back on truth – magic – everything worth having. Called the sad leftovers "reality". Lily lives like that all the time. She may have a fairy dog, but she'd never know it.'

'I bet she thinks we're a bunch of weirdos in a falling-down house,' said Saffi.

'Which she's glad she doesn't have to sell,' added Dad.

A few weeks later, life had returned more or less to normal at the B&B. Even the wallpaper stayed its habitual green. Grandma had recovered from her fall and was back to her bustling self, though she had sworn off baking. Grandad must have wanted to make amends for the True deal for he threw himself into various projects to help people, including Mr Lythe.

The feud between the two families was well and truly

over. The Trues had already invited the Lythes to dinner, a meal that passed in companionable silence as everyone battled Grandma's roast beef. That was when Mr Lythe announced that thanks to Grandad's loan, he was going to keep the park. Grandad concentrated on chewing but Saffi could tell he was pleased. She didn't know whether it was enough to offset two hundred years of greed. But she also remembered what the Lord had said in Forfeit House.

They couldn't change the past, only move forward.

Her father and brother, she was glad to see, had also recovered. Milo acquired a meditative streak after his encounter with the Lady; Saffi sometimes wondered how much of his trip to the fairy world he remembered. But he seemed content, pursuing his fossil finds with gusto. Most importantly, he hadn't told a single lie since their return.

As to Dad, the first thing he did was put Mum's pictures back in the stairwell. A few days later, he and Saffi cooked *tahdik* for lunch. They hadn't made the dish since Mum's illness and it was every bit as good as Saffi remembered. Grandma was initially doubtful, presented with the saffron-yellow rice in its crispy potato crust. But when she nibbled on a corner, her face changed and she helped herself to a large serving.

'Teach me how to make that, William True,' she said, 'and you'll never see toad-in-the-hole again.'

On a Wednesday soon after, about three weeks after the end of the True deal, Saffi caught a ride into Breakwell with her father, who dropped her off near Betty's tea shop. Milo didn't come with her that time, preferring to stay and write in his fossil diary.

'You go,' he said when she asked, flicking through pictures of fossils on Dad's phone. 'I can't decide if these are *Siphonia* or what.'

Saffi knew now that she could trust him. So she stepped into the tea shop that day with a light heart. Sun-catchers tinkled as she closed the door. It was one of Breakwell's rare sunny moments, blustery in the extreme. A young woman with bright blue hair stood behind the counter. But it was the familiar sight of Birdy that Saffi focussed on, smiling like a sunbeam in his tatty jacket. He had been sitting by the window and rose when she came in.

'Have you ordered yet?' she asked.

'Waiting for you,' he said. 'Want some ice cream?'

She did. They bought two cones – chocolate for him, strawberry for her – and went outside to eat, standing by the railings on the sea wall. It had become a regular pattern: they would meet up at Betty's every day or two, then take a walk on the beach or visit the fair rides. The Lady's flute might be gone but Birdy was saving up for another, a proper concert flute this time, and meant to start busking again. Their conversations always returned to magic or the other world.

'They say it's a mudslide,' he went on now, as they stood by the railing, gazing out to sea. 'Official report.'

He meant the cave. The day after their return from Forfeit House, they had walked out to it with Dad and

Milo, only to find the entire thing blocked up with sand and gravel. There was barely a seam left in the rock where the entrance had been.

'A fairy-slide, more like,' said Saffi. 'They've shut the doors.'

The mirror at home was the same, cracked and useless, the ornaments fused to the wood and blackened as if by a lightning strike. The ornament collection fared no better. All of the animal-head figurines had disappeared, while a number of others looked as if they had been smashed by a mallet. Saffi was relieved to see the end of them. As to Piccola and Mr B, she hadn't seen them at the house, though sometimes she caught a whiff of the musky smell.

It wasn't past adventures that troubled her today, though, as she stood eating her ice cream with Birdy. It was the future.

'D'you think she'll take me up on it?' she asked after a pause.

He knew who she meant. 'You invited the Fairy Queen to your home. She'll come, just to see if you're serious.'

'I feel like I invited a storm,' Saffi confessed.

'If so, it's a storm as blows away fools.' There was a twinkle in his eye. 'You know, since all that ended with the bank, my dad's had three offers on the park? Now! He said no thanks. Us Lythes are here to stay.'

'What about those flute lessons?' she asked.

Birdy's father had softened markedly since the evening with the coastguards. He had even promised his son music lessons.

'Starts on Friday.' Birdy gave a grimace. 'Don't know if I'll be any good though. Was it me that played, or the magic?'

'It's you,' Saffi assured him. 'The magic's in us.'

She meant it. The house might be back to normal, but it didn't follow that all the magic had disappeared. She had a dim sense of a world of possibility, both exhilarating and nerve-racking.

Birdy must have been asking himself the same question. 'D'you think they still report on us?' he said. 'To the Lady?'

He had his eye on two seagulls squabbling on the tea shop terrace. Nearby, a pied crow sat on the railing. When Saffi turned towards it, it gave a harsh, croaking cry. She could almost hear words. *Right! Right!*

'I bet they do.'

Birdy sighed. 'Nothing's going to be simple anymore, is it.'

Saffi agreed wholeheartedly, though she didn't say so. Three sparrows had now joined the crow. Further down the terrace, a yellow-necked gannet stalked along. When Birdy suggested a walk down to the beach, she followed him without comment. He was the one who raised the subject again as they crunched over the gleaming pebbles.

'What the Lady said, about not being *unchanged*. What did she mean?'

Saffi shrugged. 'Like you just said. Nothing's going to be the same now we've seen magic.'

But she watched him sidelong as they walked, wondering if he guessed that she was keeping information back. In fact, she knew what the Lady meant. She wanted to tell

Birdy – promised herself that she would, soon. She hadn't quite worked herself up to the point.

For something had happened to her, something that began after her return from Forfeit House and only became more apparent, day by day. She considered it later, after she and Birdy had said their goodbyes and she waited for the bus home. Fairy magic had unforeseen effects. She wasn't the same person who had stepped through the mirror on that memorable night. The Lady was right. Saffi wasn't *unchanged*.

She had been given a Gift. A proper one this time, unasked-for. Though as with all magic, it wasn't so simple. It was never so simple.

Sun, kids crying over dropped ice-cream, the burnt sugar smell of candyfloss. That was how a seaside town should be, she thought, gazing out over promenade. To everyone else, Breakwell looked ordinary. But Saffi knew fairy sprites lived under those bins. She saw one now, peeping out at her with a face like a rat's, just as she saw other creatures – beings, she grasped, who had always been there though she wasn't aware of it.

No one would have believed her if she told the truth: that boring old Breakwell was stranger than they could imagine, teeming with enchantment, miracles around every corner. Sprites skulked under bins, grinning or scowling. Birds flapped after her as if they sensed the change. But there were delights as well. Recently, Saffi had glanced over the sea wall at high tide to find a stunning creature in the water, silver-skinned with long green-grey hair. It hung there, moving its tail lazily in the current, staring up at her with liquid eyes.

It was beautiful. And terrifying. And electrifying. She wouldn't want to go back to *not* seeing that. But she also knew, deep down in her bones, that it could mean only one thing.

She would never be comfortable again.

Mum was right. She would always be two things, caught in between, neither and both. She wasn't afraid. It made her strong.

For this was the world as it truly was. Astonishing, marvellous, strange. A place of wonder and beauty, filled to the brim with magic; things both Seen and Unseen, as the Lady said. It was anything but ordinary.

And Saffi saw it. She could see it all.

Acknowledgements

This book started off as an ashtray.

My friend had come up to visit me in London. 'I have a present for you,' she said. 'We were deciding what to do with my grandmother's ornament collection – you remember the one – and found this. I thought it should come back to you.'

She handed me a small silver bowl. It looked like an ornamental ashtray. But the base was carved with an inscription in Farsi. When I looked closer, I realised that someone had welded a Qajar-era silver coin into the base of the bowl. On the other side was the classic image of the lion and sun, the symbol of Persian kings.

I did remember that ornament collection, and the visit when I was about twelve to the home of my friend's formidable Welsh grandmother. But how did a silver coin from nineteenth-century Persia find its way into her display cabinet in Wales, and in the shape of an ashtray, no less? Neither of us had an answer, but I knew there was a story there. Since I had no access to the original, I decided to make one up.

'Once upon a time, an Englishman came upon the Fairy Queen out riding on All Hallows' Eve, and asked her for wishes three.'

The problem isn't magic, of course, but the quality of our wishes. Maybe you are an ambitious fellow in Victorian England who wants to escape poverty. Maybe you do that by wishing you were a ship's captain with his own vessel and a lucrative line in trade. But that, for you, means taking something from others. You can't conceive of another way to be.

Despite her distaste, the Fairy Queen grants your desire. You pass that soul-debt on to your heirs: every generation, they face the same choice. To take or to give. Hopefully, some plucky descendant comes along to put a stop to the cycle.

What happens after we end the Faustian bargain? How do we make amends, tell a different story?

This book would not exist in any form without the razor-sharp insights of Chloe Sackur, my commissioning editor, as well as those of my agent Sara O'Keeffe, whose staunch support kept me going in the drafting trenches. The idea of writing about the experience of *unbelonging* began during my MA at Birkbeck College in 2020, when I was lucky enough to be a recipient of the Sophie Warne Bursary.

I would like to thank the whole team at Andersen Press

for producing the book of my heart – and my husband and daughter, for putting up with me while I wrote it.

Finally, I would like to thank my mother for giving me the gift of two worlds.

Stay uncomfortable.

WORLD WEAVERS

SAM GAYTON

Hush and Matilda have been hiding out in a pocket world, ever since the war started. Ever since Dustbowl fell. Ever since what happened to Ma. But when a boy with no memory crosses into their reality, the sisters must confront

their past, each other, and the intoxicating power that has torn their lives apart . . . the power known as worldweaving.

'Wildly original adventure from an author whose imagination seems boundless' *Lovereading*

9781839131264

The Secret of Splint Hall

KATIE COTTON

1945. War has ended, but for sisters Isobel and Flora, the struggles continue. They've lost their father and had their home destroyed in a bombing raid, and now they must go to live with their aunt and her awful husband Mr Godfrey in their ancestral home, Splint Hall. From the moment of their arrival it seems that this is a place shrouded in mysteries and secrets. As the girls begin to unearth an ancient myth and family secret, the adventure of a lifetime begins.

9781839131967